Amelia's Amnesia

by

Jennifer Taylor

PITTSBURGH, PENNSYLVANIA 15238

The contents of this work, including, but not limited to, the accuracy of events, people, and places depicted; opinions expressed; permission to use previously published materials included; and any advice given or actions advocated are solely the responsibility of the author, who assumes all liability for said work and indemnifies the publisher against any claims stemming from publication of the work.

All Rights Reserved
Copyright © 2020 Jennifer Taylor

No part of this book may be reproduced or transmitted, downloaded, distributed, reverse engineered, or stored in or introduced into any information storage and retrieval system, in any form or by any means, including photocopying and recording, whether electronic or mechanical, now known or hereinafter invented without permission in writing from the publisher.

RoseDog Books
585 Alpha Drive
Suite 103
Pittsburgh, PA 15222
Visit our website at *www.rosedogbookstore.com*

ISBN: 978-1-64913-021-1
eISBN: 978-1-64913-036-5

This novel is a work of fiction. All events, characters, and organizations other than those clearly in the public domain, are a product of the author's imagination.
Any resemblance to actual persons is coincidental.

Dedication
For Lance, the person who gave me confidence to do this.

Prologue

Brent

She looks as beautiful as the first day he laid eyes on her. *Amelia,* he thinks to himself. A name that rolls off the tongue. Her jet-black hair falls down her back in waves that shine in the light, with her skin being a pale complexion in comparison. Her almond shaped eyes that are a piercing green. She wears just enough rose-pink blush to show off her high cheek bones. Brent watches as she brings her coffee up to her full, lush lips. *What would it be like to kiss them,* he wonders? He thinks of moving a couple tables closer to her, so he can once again smell the floral breeze perfume she always wears but decides not to in case he gets caught. She always comes to this local coffee shop to do her work. It was how he first found her, through romantic poems. She writes them as a living, and he can't get enough of them.

Her poems are meant just for me. She was meant just for me, I know it. Pretending to be on his laptop as well, he moves down to what she's wearing. A yellow V-neck shirt with skinny jeans that are worn out with holes in them. Both fitting her hourglass shape of a body. Brent goes back to the fantasy that he has had many times about her. She is looking scandalous in her tight burgundy red dress, a slit on the left side of it. Her long, silky hair parted one way, falling over part of her face in soft curls. Wearing red glossy lipstick and a smoky eyeshadow that makes her eyes look even brighter. She's staring directly at him with a smile on her face. They sit down for dinner on a first date. They are at a seafood restaurant in the corner booth for privacy. The both of them talk about what they would name their future children, Jacklyn, Sara, and Benjamin. Not many people can talk about something so personal on a first date, but they can. The lights in the restaurant are dim, and she bites her lower lip as Brent rests his hand on her right thigh, they stop talking. Slowly they both lean into kiss, and she's the first one to close her eyes. *Amelia.*

He realizes he has been staring at her the whole time he had been dozing off and looks back at his computer so he's not to draw attention to himself. *The dream is so specific, it has to be real. We would fall in love in an instant, she'll see.* He logs onto his Facebook and searches for her page, Amelia Jones. Her name should be shown as Amelia Hall, Brent's last name. *It's okay that you don't use my last name, you haven't met me yet, so I forgive you. I'll be your husband someday, and we'll change your name.* He starts to read through her profile. She is 25 years old and is a poetic writer. She lives locally in New York and has many friends, including a fiancé. That is the one detail of Amelia's life that frustrates Brent. *He's a problem that can be fixed, a simple roadblock in the way.* When she's not posting pictures of her and her friends, she advertises her romantic poems that are posted on a different website. That is where he first read her work. Brent contemplates whether he should send her a friend request finally, but then decides against it. *The first time we meet should be in person, not online.* Her account is public, so he can snoop around whenever he wants to, no need to friend her. *I don't want us to be labeled as friends, we're meant to be so much more,* he thinks to himself.

Brent looks back up to the beautiful woman named Amelia, typing away on her laptop while drinking a caramel latte, her favorite. The urge to meet her finally makes him ache, but he continues to wait. *Not like this, it has to be perfect. I need the right moment to introduce myself.* For now, he continues to look at her from a far. Planning how he's going to make his fantasy become a reality.

1
Amelia

There is a pounding headache. I can't see, my body isn't awake, but my mind is. I start to hear a soft beeping in the background. I push myself harder to open my eyes, focusing on nothing but that. Slowly, they start to peel open. Everything is so bright, where am I? They flicker all the way open and I am in a white room with a strong scent of cleaners. It's a hospital, why am I in a hospital? Her body slowly begins to regain feeling. It's aching and she winces at the sudden change. There is something in my arm, moving her eyes down she sees an IV stuck in her. The headache comes back in full force. Reaching for her head with the other arm she feels gauze wrapped around her head. Did I get hit with something? That would explain the pounding feeling. There are scratches and bruises all over her arm. Inspecting the rest of her body, she discovers the scratches and bruises reach everywhere. What happened to me?

A nurse walks into the room. "I see your awake again Ms. Jones." The nurse is a sweet old Hispanic lady with gray, short hair. Wearing pink lipstick that shimmers, and a tad bit too heavy on the eyeliner. She is very petite and looks very fragile. Too hard of a hug might break her in half.

Ms. Jones? Suddenly she realizes she doesn't even know who she is. How does that happen? This is her body, but she feels like a total stranger in her mind. Confusion and slight panic overtake her. The nurse sees the change and rushes in to explain.

"Sweety, I'm sorry to tell you, but you were in an accident and had a head injury as a result of it. You have retrograde amnesia, or RA for short." The nurse is continuing to explain what that means, but I can't hear anything she's saying, only her mouths moving. I have amnesia. There was an accident? Fear that this could be permanent overtakes her. "What's my name?"

"Your name is Amelia Jones."

"What accident was I in?"

"It was a hiking accident with your fiancé. You took quite a fall."

I have a fiancé? She looks and sees a ring on her finger, which confirms it. She doesn't remember herself or anybody else in her life. Now that she thinks about it, she doesn't remember anything about her life. She is a blank page. There are a million questions running through her head. A head that suddenly can't take it and begins to ache further. Wincing harder this time, I try to relax and worry about the details later.

The nurse looks concerned now. "Sweety, you need to rest and not get too worked up. I know this has got to be a lot to process, but your brain is trying to heal right now. As well as the rest of your body. Thank goodness you didn't suffer any broken bones or fractures. If you ask me, you were very fortunate. You've been fading in and out on us for four days now, so this is actual progress." The nurse smiles at Amelia and starts checking her vitals. She then pulls out a clipboard and starts recording everything down.

Looking at Amelia again, "Looks like we have to change your bandages dear." She puts the clipboard back and begins with the gauze covering the top of her head.

"Can I see what it looks like?"

The nurse presses her lips together and her eyebrows arch up in a' worried fashion. "I'm not sure if you would want to see how you look right now Ms. Jones. You had a long fall and you look different, don't want anything to raise your stress levels again."

"I can handle it, please. I don't even know how I'm supposed to look." Giving the nurse a pleading look. I can't even place my identity with a face. After some hesitation, the nurse gives her an expression of sorrow, but also understanding. "Okay sweety, but remember, you're still healing. This look is only temporary." Amelia nods with a half-smile. Finally getting to see who she is. The nurse walks over to a bin and grabs a blue mirror with a handle. The reflection side is pressed against the nurse's chest before she slowly stretches it out towards her. She grabs it with the arm that doesn't have needles in it and turns it over.

She gasps. It was worse than she thought. It looks like I was in an MMA fight, and I lost badly. Under both of her eyes was a plum purple color mixed with a navy blue, one of her eyes slightly swollen. Small cuts ran all over her face and one big one over her hair line that was closed with a few stitches. Her lips were pale, swollen,

Amelia's Amnesia

and busted open at the bottom. Random blotches of red and brown bruises spread across her face, including her cheekbone, chin, and forehead. Looking back to her eyes, there were bags under them, making her look old and tired. A little tear ran down her face as she was looking at the new her.

"Again honey, this is only temporary." The nurse said as she quickly snatched the mirror from her, regretting the decision of letting Amelia see herself in the first place. Amelia seeing the image of her face in her head now, wonders how bad her body looks under the gown.

"How long until I heal?" she wonders out loud.

"That's hard to tell, everybody is different. Personally, you look much better now compared to when we first saw you. The doctor said you should be able to leave soon as well."

Wow, how bad was I when they first saw me? Is she just saying that to make me feel better? Another headache comes back to remind her it's still there.

"Is there anything I can have for the pain." Amelia's face showing what she's feeling.

The nurse checks her watch. "Of course sweety, right on cue actually. I'll get you fixed up right away. Would you like to see your fiancé now? He should be done talking to the police by now and waiting outside for -"

"Wait, the police? Was I attacked?" Her eyes getting big at the thought of someone doing this to her. Was someone trying to kill me? "No, no! They all believe it was an accident, but they just want to make sure of that dear, no need to worry." The nurse said with the sincerest smile she could give at the moment.

"Thank God! I guess I could meet my fiancé. Who is he?" Maybe he could help her with all this memory loss. "His name is Michael sweety, I'll send him!"

Just before the nurse left, she had one more question, "Wait… I forgot my name again." She looked down feeling helpless and ashamed for some reason. I should at least be able to remember my own name. I've only had it for my entire life. The nurse smiles politely, "It's Amelia dear, if you forget again, you can look right on your wristband to help you." Amelia looks at the wristband the nurse is pointing to and feels relieved that she has some type of reminder of who she is. Feeling better she tells the nurse, "Okay, I'm ready to see my fiancé, Michael."

2
Michael

"Are you Michael Williams?" A detective asked him. The detective was a tall man in his forties with bags under his eyes, showing how tired he must be from working late nights as a cop. With him was a younger woman in her thirties with a dark complexion and dark brown eyes. "Yes, I'm Michael."

"Hi Michael, I'm Detective Burgh and this is my partner, Detective Smith." She puts her hand up to greet Michael, and he shakes it while giving her a respectful nod. Detective Burgh continues, "May we go in a more private area, we have a few questions for you."

"That's fine by me." He follows them back into an empty room that was left alone for them. The room was bleak and white with only one closed at the top of the wall where all you could see is the red bricks that belong to the building next door. All he smells here are cleaners and polluted air. He misses the fresh air he gets where he lives. The only time he goes out to the city is when he goes to work, besides that he's at home in the more country area where neighbors aren't in your bubble and you can see animals prancing around. The whole time he has been worried about Amelia. Is she alive? How badly was she injured? When can I see her again? As he was scared for her well-being, he was also a little relieved in a way that her memory was erased.

No one knew yet, but Amelia and Michael had been going through a rough patch. So rough, she had been considering leaving. He almost shivered at that thought but stopped himself knowing there were two people looking at him. At least we can start fresh and rebuild the relationship without her knowing how bad we were. We can stay engaged and I'll have a second chance to make everything up to her.

"So, let's start." Said Detective Burgh "The hospital told us you and your fiancée Amelia had been hiking before she had been injured."

"That's right."

"Where were you two hiking?"

"The trail just south of here. We live in a wooded area and usually walk together around there but wanted to see a new setting this time."

"So, you both were not familiar with the trail?"

"No sir, the first time we had been there."

Detective Smith starts writing frantically in a notepad, recording everything on paper. After a moment Detective Burgh continues, "What happened to cause Ms. Jones injuries?" Michael wishes she was Mrs. Williams. He was more than ready for marriage, was ready for it a year ago, but Amelia needed more time to be sure. Hopefully after this life changing event, she'll be ready now.

"Well I wasn't there to see specifically how things happened. After a little bit of time being on the trail, I had to use the restroom since I drank a lot of water. Since there's no restrooms on the trail, I walked off some to find a place where Amelia wouldn't have to see me. After I found a spot and did my business, I heard a shriek that sounded like her. I ran back to the trail and saw some scuff marks and a tree with a bit of blood on it. The trail was going up a hill where we were at, so I looked down and saw her body unconscious at the bottom of it. It was quite a drop so I was terrified that she might be dead. There was blood still coming out of her, mostly from her head. I sprinted down the hill towards her. After I found her pulse and checked her limbs for any sprains or broken bones, I picked her up and rushed her back to our car. Googled the nearest hospital and sped her over here."

"Was there anybody else on the trail?"

"No sir, at least none that I could see. We had been walking alone for a while."

"You're sure that there was nobody else behind you or in front of you two at the trail?"

"It was just us, I guess not a lot of people visit that trail."

Detective Burgh pauses again, then resumes. "Does Ms. Jones have any enemies?"

"No, everybody loves her. The thing that drew me to her was her kindness and understanding of people."

"Has she complained of any stalkers to you? Maybe a certain person or car that frequently follows her around?"

"No, nothing that she's ever told me about."

"Has she gotten any threats recently or in the past. Text messages or letters?"

"She hasn't, nothing."

Amelia's Amnesia

Detective Burgh moves on, "We were also informed that Ms. Jones phone was no longer on her."

"Yeah, it took me a moment to realize that since I was so focused on her. Amelia's shorts had small pockets and her phone was sticking halfway out of them the whole time. My guess is it got stuck in a crevice somewhere down the hill or got lost in the river next to her and went down stream." Michael admits to himself that even that sounds weird to him. It should be somewhere. Phones don't just disappear.

Detective Smith looks up, a bit confused at his remark but says nothing and writes it down. "Alright." Detective Burgh states. "That's about all the questions we have for now. We will look for her phone and will inform you if we find it."

"Are you going to question Amelia as well?"

"Usually we would question Ms. Jones as well as all witnesses, but in this rare case we're not going to worry about that. Considering that your fiancée isn't sure of her name and no one else was at the scene, it won't do us any good to get her side, seeing that she doesn't have one. If she regains her memory of that day, we would like you to contact us right away." Detective Burgh hands Michael his card with his name and number. "This checks out to be an accidental fall. We will contact you with any new findings, but for now you are good to go. We are sorry of the situation that has taken place right now." Detective Smith looks at him with concerned eyes, "I hope your fiancée gets better."

"Thank you both, and I will be sure to call if I think of anything else or if she remembers." Michael lifts the card up with his hand showing that he knows what to do if something comes up.

"Let's get out of here." Detective Burgh says towards Detective Smith. "You are welcome to go back to the waiting room Mr. Williams."

Michael nods and makes his way back. Just in time to see Nurse Ruby from earlier who has been checking on Amelia. She is searching for him and finds him as he walks towards her. "Anything new?" He asks her. "Yes Mr. Williams, great news! Amelia is finally staying awake and she wants to talk to you."

Michael becomes ecstatic at what the nurse says and can't hide the big grin that has formed on his face. "That's amazing! Let's go." They both walk fast towards Amelia's room, Michael excited to finally be reunited with her. *This is my chance to start over and do everything right.*

3
Brent

Brent is back at the hospital. He's been coming back and forth for four days now. Walking through the hallways to eavesdrop, he has discovered that Amelia is doing better now. At least she's okay now. *I haven't lost her.* He so badly wants to go in her room to check on her, see how cute she is when she's sleeping, but knows he can't be caught. *There would be too many questions that I couldn't answer. I can't have her see me yet, not like this, not in a hospital.* His thinking comes to a stop when he sees two detectives approach Michael. Obviously for questioning. As they leave to go back to another room, Brent's curiosity gets the best of him and he follows behind with a distance, so they don't see him through the turns they take. They end up in a private room. Thankfully the door is just a little cracked so he can hear their conversation. As he's listening, Michael's voice angers him. *Why does he get to be with her? He's no good for an angel like Amelia. She didn't seem that happy with him. I could make her happy. Be there to do everything and anything to make her happy. She would have a smile on her face every time she saw me.*

As their conversation furthers, he flashes back to how he was there on the hiking path with them. There were lots of trees and bushes, so staying hidden was easy. Amelia's hair was in a long ponytail. Waves like a wild ocean swooping down her back as she walked. Her full lips were a natural pink and her lashes were still unbelievably long and dark without any mascara. Her shorts were tight and fit her curves nicely. She complained to Michael about how she needed new ones soon since her rear hung out just a bit at the ends, but Brent didn't complain, he just took in her beauty. She was wearing a mossy green tank top that hugged her slender stomach and natural size D chest. He knows what size she is, because he's been in her room before, seen her clothes and fittings. I need to know what sizes she is, so I can buy her clothes when she's mine. He knows what happened on the trail. It wasn't supposed to happen like that. The whole thing was an accident, but he can't say that. He can't go to the detective and explain what happened, he would for sure be in trouble. Brent instead just keeps listening to the detectives and Michael talk.

They get to the question of the phone missing. Both the detectives say how they're going to go back to look for it. They're not going to find it, because it's not there. It didn't get stuck in a rock or fall into the river. He then hears them wrapping up, calling it an accidental fall, like she tripped. He knows she didn't but begins to head back to the waiting room before they do. Soon she'll be out of here and back to her old routine. Everything will go back to normal, and I can continue on how I'm going to meet her, properly.

He sees the old nurse walking around, surely looking for Michael. He wishes it was him who could go see her. Brent wonders why the nurse looks so eager, she's practically on her toes looking for Michael. What happened, is she finally up? Can I hear her voice again? A voice that he's missed, sweet and innocent, with a hint of a seductive tone. No wonder why men want her, she's absolutely perfect, but she's already meant for me. I have to fight the posers off of her. She doesn't need them, or Michael, she needs me.

The nurse finds Michael and tells him how Amelia is awake and talking. I look down and smile under my cap. She's up and doing better. She's a fighter. With no more being said, they move back to her room and I wait two more minutes before getting up and roaming the halls again so I can see her. She's healed well and will be back out in the real world soon, where our fate awaits.

4
Amelia

She looks at Michael for the first time. He is a handsome man as he looks right into her eyes. He is an average height man, slender with a bit of muscle. He has an olive color tan with dark brown eyes, almost black. His hair is a dirty blond, browner in some places. It's cut and slicked back neatly. His face has sharp angles with a masculine chin and bold nose. His eyes are big like hers and his eyebrows are thick and brown. Michael is wearing baggy dark jeans with a light blue t-shirt that's fitting, yet baggy as well. She doesn't mind staring at him.

"Hey Amelia, how are you?"

"Better once the nurse gave me something for the pain."

Michael's eyes suddenly get watery. She's confused on why and is afraid she's said something wrong. "What is it? Was it something I said?"

"No, I just haven't heard you talk in days and truly miss it. I miss you and you're finally here, back." He says and turns away to regain his emotions. For a moment, she doesn't know what to say. There are so many questions, she doesn't even know where to start.

"What happened to me?"

"You tripped and fell when I went to use the restroom. You hit your head on a tree and the doctor says you most likely rolled down the hill the rest of the way. Since you took a large blow to the head, it gave you amnesia." Amelia touches her head where the stitches are. Michael then takes her hand from her head and holds it firmly.

"Where are we? I know we're in a hospital right now, but where do we live?"

"We live in New York. Right now, we're in the city, but our house is in the country area of New York." He tells her. New York? Have I always lived here?

"Where are my parents? Can I see them as well?" With this question, Michael looks down. She knows there won't be a good answer to this.

"Your parents aren't in your life. Haven't been since you were two. Both of your parents were alcoholics, who were addicted to meth, as well as made it. A neighbor complained one day, and social services came in to take you. Your grandma claimed you."

"So, where is she?" Amelia is still a bit hopeful for having any family.

Michael is still looking at the floor. "She died three years ago. About a year before we met. You moved from Pennsylvania to New York, because you were heartbroken about it."

"What about a grandpa?" Her eyebrows are pinched together.

"Your grandma was a single mother. You told me how she would always tell you that she didn't need a man, and that you didn't either. That you both had girl power." He finally looks up at her and checks on her. Amelia is hurt, seeing that there is no family, she wants to move onto a different subject instead of dwelling on this.

"What about any friends?"

"You have a few from back in college, but don't see them often since they still live in Pennsylvania." At this she brightens up a bit. There are more people who can help put her life back together.

"Can I text or call them? Where's my phone?" Amelia looks around the room, seeing if it could be resting on a seat or table.

"Your phone was lost on the trail, but don't worry, I'll get you a new one soon." He looks at her more with a stern expression, reassuring that he will fix that problem. Seeing a dead end to this conversation, she moves on.

"What was my job before this? I must have done something, especially since I went to college."

"You majored in English and became a romance poet for a site that paid you for your poems. You were really good at it."

"Were?"

"Well yeah, you quit recently so we could start planning our wedding and kids." Michael is hoping they could speed the process up after everything that's happened. He doesn't want to lose her again.

"Um, kids? We could put a hold on that, right?" She looks at him concerned. I feel like I just met this guy, he can't be serious about kids right now. I didn't even consider putting sex as an option at this point.

"Of course! I know you're going to need time to get everything back on

Amelia's Amnesia

track." A wave of relief washes over her.

"How old am I?" She goes back to more basic questions.

"You're 25 and I'm 34."

So, he's older than me. She would have guessed she was thirty with the exhausted bags under her eyes "What year is it? What month?"

Michael continues with easy patience. "It's currently 2019, right now its September. Soon it'll be Fall season."

Does she like the Fall? She'll have to wait for it to come. Amelia moves back to the career questions. "What do you do if I don't have to work?" It must be something good, I don't imagine many poets get paid a lot.

"I work as a plastic surgeon, a pretty good one, so I have to drive out to the city. Business is doing well right now." Michael smiles at his accomplishments. Amelia can't help but wonder, "Did I get anything –"

"No, you didn't get any plastic surgery, you're not into that type of stuff." He smiles lightly at her. She feels relieved. This body is all me.

"What am I like as a person." She wants to know more complex questions now.

"You are a beautiful person on the inside and out. You always light up the room, no matter where you're at. People steal glances at you all the time. You are very passionate about your writing, and I respect that you do what you love. You're nice to everyone around you, no matter who it is. People see you as very innocent, but you can be naughty towards me at the right times." At this Amelia blushes hard. Michael continues, "You're smart and are amazing at reading people. How they feel, and who they are as a person. You surround yourself around good influences and show how much you love me with the time we spend together." She can see why she is with Michael, so sweet and patient. They are a good match.

"Come on babe, the doctor told me you are good to go home, and I don't want you to be kept up in this hospital any more than what you need to be." Before Amelia can respond, he calls in the nurse and says they are ready to go. The nurse looks at her before she says anything, and Amelia gives a small smile and nod in approval. The nurse smiles. "Of course sweety, now before you go." She reaches into her pocket and hands Michael a card. "We would like her to see this shrink about her amnesia. See if he can jog her memory a bit."

Michael looks at the card and puts it in his jean's pocket. "Thanks, we'll call him, but for now I would like her to rest a bit more before putting her into any new situations."

"Sure, hope you get all better honey!" The nurse says as she turns to her. What a sweet lady. With that, Amelia starts to change in some jeans and a shirt that Michael brought over from their house. Michael gets a wheelchair that is mandatory for her to leave in and he pushes her to their silver SUV. She gets in and he smiles before he turns the key and puts it into drive. There are so many things I'm excited to find out about, but first, I am glad to be away from the cleaner smell and back to fresh air. Amelia smiles as the hospital becomes smaller in the rearview mirror and they head closer to the house she is currently living in. She is making progress.

5
Amelia

As we approach the house, I can see the long yard we have. There's about half a mile of yard around the house, before it turns into the woods where the trees take over. She looks back at the house and admires it. The siding is dark oak wood, with a black tile roof. Half of the house is made of glass walls, pointing towards the main entrance to the woods. Amelia thinks of the gorgeous view they must have every morning walking down to the kitchen, watching the sun rise above the trees. She's also relieved that their neighbors are far away, with half of their house clear and in plain sight to the outside world. Amelia already knows that she's going to love this place all over again. Michael opens the black garage doors and slides in their SUV smoothly. Once parked, she steps out and lets him lead her into the house. They end up in the living room first. The room they have is spacious and crazy to her. The ceiling hangs high and there are no doors separating the rooms. There is a huge, slim TV hanging on the wall and long, black leather couches that look stuffed beyond belief for comfort when you sit. The carpet is a classic beige color and is spotless as well. This place looks like it's barely lived in. Amelia looks to her left and sees where the glass window starts in the kitchen area. She walks over to get a better look at it as Michael silently follows. Observing her emotions and astonishment.

  The table and cabinets are made of the same wood as the outside of their house but looks more modern. Which one of us chose the furniture and décor of this place? All the plates, cups, and silverware are matching and spotless. There are green plants everywhere. She walks up to a hanging one that stretches out of its bowl to feel if it's real, it is. They all must be real. It smells earthy in here. She then turns her head to the right and sees the stairs, they make a long way upstairs. "Go check it out." Michael nudges her with his elbow, a quirky smile on his face. She goes up the steps with him behind her, taking in her curves that he dearly missed. She finds three different rooms up there, all the doors closed. The first one to the left is an office. It must be for him. There's a huge desk that takes up a good amount of space and a bookshelf that covers the right part of the wall. Behind the desk is a huge bay window, so again any person in there can appreciate the view.

Stepping out of that room, Amelia walks across the hall to the next room on the left. She assumes it must be their room, and it's a master bedroom. Their bed is a king size one with red silk covers. The posts reaching up high on each corner. To the left she noticed another door, and her curiosity took over. She opened the door to a walk-in closet. On the left was his clothes, and on the right was hers. We both have a good amount of clothing to choose from. She closes the door and sees another door across the room in the corner. That door leads her into a master bathroom that had a stand-in shower and jacuzzi tub that could easily fit a couple of people. In this room, there were roses that lined up on the bedroom window. Amelia walks to go see the last room on the right, but Michael grabs her arm before she steps across the hall and pulls her back into their bedroom.

"That's just a boring guest bedroom, nothing exciting to see in there." She thinks about still going to see it anyways, but then changes her mind since he didn't make a big deal about it. He caresses a loose strand of hair behind her ear and she looks into his eyes. They show how much he truly adores her, and she begins to feel warm inside. "I have a surprise for you."

"Oh, you do?" A surprise? This is already a lot to take in, what more could he be planning?

"Yeah, while you were getting better at the hospital today, I had a chef come in and prepare us a romantic meal. I believe it's still in the oven to keep warm. Put this on for me and then join me downstairs in the kitchen. Your make-up is in the bathroom cabinet to the right, under the sink." He walked into the closet and pulled out a lovely black cocktail dress. She looked at the tag. I'm a size four. Michael continued. "We'll have a date right inside our house tonight. Kind of like a welcome home gift." He wraps his arms around hers and she feels how firm his muscles are around her. She tilts her head to the side and says, "Whatever you want." With that, his smile becomes bigger to where his white teeth show, and he steps out to give her privacy while she changes.

6
Brent

She's finally out of the hospital and back home. Brent was worried that it might start looking suspicious if he kept going to the hospital but didn't actually visit anyone. Here in the woods it was easy. It's not like a waiting room, the only things to see me around here are animals. They have half of their house made of glass to enjoy the view, and Brent enjoys the view he gets too. Besides the glass walls, they also have huge windows, so it makes it easier for him to see through the other rooms as well. He doesn't just want to see Amelia in the kitchen and living room, he wants to see her everywhere. The only difficulty Brent finds is the spacious lawn keeps him from getting any closer. I would stick out like a sitting duck in the freshly cut lawn. He had to purchase some pricey binoculars, but it was worth it to him. They were the good kind used for hunting. He liked to think sometimes he was hunting her like she was a deer, about to be his prize.

He watched as she walked around the whole house in amazement. It's not that good, he wouldn't have all of that if he wasn't a plastic surgeon. She's not the type of person who needs the finer things in life, she would be just as happy living with me. Feeling a bit jealous at Amelia's reactions towards Michael, he keeps watching.

He sees her go through each room, but the last one. Is there a reason why Michael didn't want to show her that one? I wonder what he told her that room was, probably just a spare one. Brent knows what room that is. It's definitely not a spare, but he's glad they didn't go into that one. She shouldn't be introduced to that room ever again. He breathes a sigh of relief when they stop at the bedroom. Brent knows it's only a matter of time until Michael opens that room back up to Amelia again though. I need to see her before that happens.

Paying closer attention to what they're doing, Michael hands her a black dress to put on before he makes his way out of the room and downstairs to the kitchen. As Michael takes out dinner plates for the both of them, Brent focuses on what Amelia is doing. Thinking she's alone, she begins to change clothes. He focuses his binoculars in view as she starts with her shirt. She crosses her arms at the bottom of her white plain shirt and lifts up. Her slender stomach comes into view, then her beige bra. Brent prefers to see her in her lace bras but won't be picky. She throws her shirt into the hamper next to the door and moves to her skinny jeans. She unbuttons those with ease, and bends over as she slides them down to her ankles to pick them off. He can see the black cotton thong with a pink heart that's sewn in above her bare rear. It's smooth and perfectly round. She always wears thongs, and when it's not thongs, she wears G-strings. Always.

Next, he watches her as she moves into the bathroom to do her make-up. She doesn't want the make-up to get on her clothes, so she frequently puts it on in her underwear. It must be a natural reaction for her to do that since she's still doesn't remember much. Brent looks at her sort through her bag to see what she has, then chooses to stick with eyeliner, mascara, and the rose-pink blush he loves so much. She carefully puts it on, especially with the eyeliner and her slightly swollen eye, and studies herself for a moment. She's gorgeous even with the cuts and bruises, Michael doesn't deserve that.

She walks back into the bedroom and Brent steadily follows with the binoculars. He's become a master at doing that. She returns for the dress and puts it on carefully, not to smudge her make-up. She soon realizes she can't wear the dress with a bra. Amelia reaches behind her for the hooks, and Brent focuses in on her even more. These are some of his favorite moments. Just as she got the bra to unclip, she turns and all that shows is her back. He curses under his breath that he couldn't see more today, but he knew he would have more chances in the future. Brent puts the binoculars back up. He watches the dress slowly form over her body and she smooths it out with her hands. It's very low cut in the front, so she fills in the bare space with a small heart shaped diamond necklace she found in the closet. Amelia teases her hair a bit before opening the door to head to the kitchen. Michael is waiting for her with a bottle of wine. Brent becomes furious. She isn't his, she's mine. Fate brought us together, not her and Michael. He stops watching and takes a deep breath. Soon enough I'll let her see what a mistake she's making, soon.

7
Amelia

She walks down the steps and watches Michael absorb in her beauty. She blushes and finds herself feeling shy suddenly, like this is her very first date with this handsome man. He has a bottle of white wine on the table and two glasses that already have a pour in them. Do I drink? I must have occasionally, he wouldn't have gotten wine if I didn't. As she reaches the bottom of the steps, she sees the dinner the chef prepared. Lamb chops with Caesar salads and bread sticks. The smell makes her mouth water. She didn't realize how hungry she's been. Michael pulls out a chair for her. "I hope you like it, I asked the chef to surprise us."

"I love it, this is so much! You really went all out."

"Anything for my baby." He looks like he's about to kiss her, then stops himself, remembering their situation. Michael gives Amelia her part of dinner, then serves himself before he sits down. Immediately she digs into her food and savors the flavors. This chef sure did an amazing job.

Michael who hasn't begun looks at her, "How is it?" She feels her face heat with embarrassment, digging into her food like nobodies there.

"It's really good, you should try it."

"You don't have to be embarrassed Amelia. I'm your fiancé, I've seen you in every way, shape, and form. This isn't the first time I've seen you really hungry. This must be a step up from the hospital food." He smirks. She starts laughing and feels like the awkward vibe was broken. She looks at him drink some wine and he looks back over at her.

"What is it?"

She puts a light smile on her face. "How did we first meet?"

He puts his drink down. "It's actually kind of funny how we met. One day after work I went to a restaurant and sat at the bar area to relax a little before I went home. After about fifteen minutes of being there, you scooch up next to me in a hurry for something. Before I can even say hello you ask me for a favor." He starts to laugh, and she smiles. He has such a quirky laugh that I'm already hooked to. "You were a beautiful sight to see, and since I didn't want you to leave, I said of course. There was a creepy guy in his fifties, with a bald spot, who was constantly hitting on you. You thought if we pretended to be together, he would leave you alone. Instantly you made my night more exciting. It wasn't that hard to pretend that I was with you, I constantly had my arm around your waist. Even after the guy left, you didn't leave, you stayed at the bar and asked for some wine. This is actually the same wine that you ordered." He holds up the bottle of white wine on the table.

Amelia is surprised. "You remember something so little like that?"

"It wasn't little to me. We talked for hours about everything. I couldn't help myself from cracking jokes about the unfortunate guest you had to deal with, and you just kept laughing the whole time. At the end when it was time to go, we stared at each other for a moment before we kissed. It was then that I knew I wanted to have you in a real relationship. We've been together ever since." He reaches for her hand and cups it in his. It truly feels like a romantic moment for her. I really met the right guy. She has a lot more to learn but is comfortable being around him. She feels safe.

Now feeling playful, Amelia flicks a piece of lettuce at him. It plops right on his forehead and she holds in a laugh when it sticks there. Blinking in disbelief, Michael asks, "Is that lettuce you just threw at me?" She nods with a devious smile and in return he rips off a small piece of breadstick and throws food right back at her. It's on now, fair game. One by one, they both throw food carelessly across the table. Mouths open laughing, a crouton lands into her mouth and Michael cheers while putting his arms up in a goal sign. Wanting to one up him in this battle, Amelia reaches for a whole breadstick. He follows and the throwing turns into a sword fight.

Blocking and swinging, they're both competitive on the table at this point. She gets an idea of how to get an advantage on him. She grabs a handful of Caesar salad from the bowl and throws the leafy greens at his face as a distraction. He puts his hands to his face distinctively, and she jabs him in the stomach with her bread. Feeling victorious, she puts her hands up, claiming she's the winner. Michael decides to take the bowl and dump the salad over her, like how players dump water over their coach at the end of a game.

Amelia's Amnesia

Being covered in food, she hugs him and pulls him down from on his knees to laying over her. Their laughing stops as they just stare into each other's eyes. "I could get used to spending time with you." She says, taking her thumb to wipe some meat sauce off his cheek.

"Good, because I don't plan on going anywhere."

"I can see why I chose to sit next to you that day."

Michael cocks his head to the side. "Oh really, why's that?"

"You have charisma, something that radiates off of you." She feels intimate with him now.

"Was it like a magnet that attracted you." He laughs.

"You could say that, I'm just glad I approached you first. Before any other women did."

"I'm sure if there was a crowd of women around me, I would still choose you." His light humor was gone, replaced with a more serious voice.

They stared at each other even longer this time. Silence between them, but it wasn't awkward. Amelia cupped her hand around his strong jaw line. He is quite a view, I'm really going to have to get used to this. Michael takes his hand and puts his fingers through her hair. He leans down slowly, making sure she's ready, and they kiss. It's first a light peck before she brings him back down for a more passionate one. They stay that way for what seems awhile, until he pulls away to look back into her green eyes.

"So, who's going to clean up this mess?" She laughs and lightly slaps his arm.

"I'm kidding, we'll both do it. Then I'll start the jacuzzi with some suds you can soak in to relax." He pecks her one more time on the lips before getting off the table. She sits up and looks at him roll up his sleeves. How was I so lucky to end up with him that night, my knight in shining armor.

8
Michael

Last night was perfect. It was almost like the first night we met, but better. I had her all to myself. Michael wakes up with a smile, turning and looking at Amelia who was still sleeping. It was almost a week of him waking up alone. He missed having her in his bed, seeing her beautiful face every morning. He wishes he could spend the whole day with her again but can't keep missing work. He still has to make money for the both of them, especially since she won't be working anymore. Michael wonders how long they're going to have to postpone on having kids. At least she's still here, it could be worse he thinks. He slowly slides out of bed, so he doesn't disturb her. She was practically knocked out after her bath in the jacuzzi. His pajamas are a pair of boxers with a grey tank top on. She wore a short, purple night gown. It slid up a bit as she turned over, so he could see her thong and everything else around it. Man, I love her. He walks into the master bathroom to start the shower.

  As he's washing himself, he pictures the times she would join him in there before he went off to work. Those would be the best days. She would pretend to be sleeping, then surprise him as she walks in the bathroom naked. Opening the door to his shower and letting herself in. As he finishes up, he turns off the water and steps back into reality. We'll eventually get back to that, it'll just take some time.

  He begins looking at what clothes he's going to wear today and what clients he has. Sometimes he flirts with the cute ones around his age, but that's as far as it goes. It's totally harmless, not like I'm cheating or anything on her, it's just me having a little bit of fun. It won't hurt her if she doesn't know about it. He never takes it any further, that would be completely unethical of him as a doctor. He wouldn't throw his license away over some cute patients. Michael chooses a white dress shirt and black slacks, nice and simple.

He walks downstairs to the kitchen and starts breakfast. Usually Amelia wakes up in the mornings and makes him breakfast, but that will have to be another transition he will have to wait for. For him, he makes sunny side up eggs with sausages, and pulls a strawberry yogurt out the fridge. For Amelia, he makes a cheese, ham, and spinach omelet with some French toast on the side. As if the food was calling her, she walks down the steps.

He turns to her as he's finishing her meal. "Good morning babe, just in time. Take a seat." She does as he says.

"It smells great. Thanks for breakfast."

"It tastes better when you make it, but I try my best." He shows a light smile at her.

"Do I usually cook breakfast?"

"Usually you cook every meal since I go out to work."

Amelia is taken a little bit back by this. "I used to work too."

"Yeah, but it's different, you know."

"I guess." He's sees her brush it off and bite into her food.

"I got to go back to work today, so you can explore more inside the house and outside the house." He points to the woods outside the glass wall. "Don't go too far though since you don't remember the path."

"Will do." She smiles with a closed mouth, while chewy on her omelet.

After he finishes his breakfast, he gets all his stuff together and kisses her on the forehead before he leaves to the garage. While driving to the city, he envisions his day. I have a total of five patients today. Afterwards I need to pick up Amelia's pain pills and think of what I'm going to make for dinner tonight. It'll be nice when she starts taking over the cooking again. I'll make sure of it, it's the least she could do since she'll be home all day now.

After finally getting to work in the city, he breathes in the air and misses the fresh air at his house. Michael walks in the building, puts on his Doctor's coat, and prepares for his first consultation with a patient. She's pretty cute, but also flat chested. He can already tell what this lady is coming in for. Maybe he can have some fun being flirtatious today. Let me see how she is once she's in here. He tells the receptionist to let his first patient in.

9
Amelia

After breakfast, she tries to find what she can do first for today. They only have one car, so she's stuck at the house. It doesn't make a lot of sense that we only have one car. What if I want to go somewhere? Obviously I wouldn't right now, but I must have wanted to leave the house sometimes in the past, right? What if I needed something when Michael was at work? Does he usually drive me everywhere, doesn't seem very efficient. She first decides to look at the food they eat since she's already in the kitchen. Opening the fridge and cabinets, Amelia sees all fresh foods and spices. Looks like everything is cooked from scratch, it tastes better that way. She puts everything back where she found it, she can tell Michael might be a borderline clean freak. She walks over to the living room area. Doesn't seem like it's lived in. Besides the two long couches and TV, there's a fairly small wood table that holds the remote and a couple of magazines in alphabetical order. She picks up the magazines to see some stuff they read. Some of them are medical themed, beauty, fashion, and political ones. They're average type ones. Amelia puts them back in alphabetical order and decides to head upstairs.

The first room closest to her is the office, so she stops in there. A lot of the books in there are classic novels. This is something she might read in her free time. Did she do that before? She moves over to the desk. It is a modern touch screen computer that's password protected and barely any utensils on the desk. The rest of the stuff must be in the drawers of the desk. Amelia is curious to look but doesn't want to snoop through his personal work papers. She's about to leave, seeing nothing more, until something stands out to her. On his desk is a business card, one that's not his. She picks it up to look at it. Dr. Mart, a shrink. Amelia remembers the nurse giving this to Michael before they left. This guy might be able to really help me. She desperately wants her old memories back. She picks up his landline office phone since she still doesn't have her cell phone and dials the number.

"Hello, Dr. Mart's office, how may I help you." A young woman's voice answers.

"Hi, my name is Amelia Jones, I was recently in the hospital for retrograde amnesia and they gave me Dr. Mart's business card to see him." She feels a bit nervous, not knowing what to expect from a shrink.

"I'm sorry to hear that. Let me see his openings." There's a small pause. "Okay, Dr. Mart can see you next week, Wednesday at 12:00?"

"Yeah that's fine, thank you!"

"You're welcome, bye."

"Bye." Amelia feels like she's making more progress. She'll have to find out how she's going to get there. I'll find a way, she thinks to herself. Seeing that there's nothing else in the office, she moves on. Amelia has already been in the bedroom a couple of times, so she eyes the guest bedroom. Maybe she can take a look at it now since Michael isn't here. She walks to the end of the hallway and reaches for the knob. It's locked from the outside. That's weird, why would the door be locked from the outside instead of the inside? What if someone was in there when it's locked, they wouldn't be able to get out. It looks like the door unlocks with a key. She has no idea where it would be, so her adventure ends here. Thinking she has yet to step outside, she goes in their bedroom to change from her pajamas to clothes. She puts on a buttoned pink tank top and some regular jean shorts. Amelia steps out the house and goes to the main opening to the woods.

It's dense with trees and she can hear the sounds of birds and woodpeckers in different directions. Suddenly she gets an aching feeling in her head and a picture begins to form. She's been in here before, lots of times actually. A little further out, there's a stream with a tiny waterfall that ends in a natural pond. she loves to go by there and take a dip in the pond that's big enough for a group of people. Seeing the path in her head, she trusts her instincts and walks in further. After five minutes, going past a big rock and a tree that's fallen, Amelia finds her favorite spot in the woods. Sitting on one of the rocks, she stares at the miniature waterfall. She remembers how Michael and she found this spot together one day. There wasn't anything in the water, so they decided to go skinny dipping. She liked coming here alone as well to think about her poetry. Feeling a bit hot from the summer heat that still lingers before Fall, she thinks about taking a dip in the pond again like she has several times. Not bringing a bathing suit out with her, she peeks around to make sure none of the neighbors are out taking a long walk like she is. Seeing no one around, she begins to undress and place her clothes on the rock she was sitting on.

Amelia's Amnesia

The water in the pond is clear enough to see the smooth rocks that cover the bottom and sides of it. It's cool to the touch as she dips her toe in first. Amelia slowly steps in, careful not to slip. Once she's fully in the pond, the water reaches up to her ribs. Feeling refreshed she traces her fingers on top of the water, seeing the lines and ripples it makes. Suddenly she hears a branch snap. Gasping, she dips into the water, only keeping her face out, and slides over to a bigger rock to try and hide. I thought there was no one else here. Did a neighbor come by while I wasn't paying attention? What if someone saw me, would they come over? She slowly looks over the rock, only keeping the top of her head visible over it. Scanning the area more carefully this time, her eyes land on a female dear. It's eating a patch of moss while looking back at her. She stands up and relaxes her shoulders in relief. It was silly to think anyone else would be here. Michael told me the neighbors were far away.

Moving back into the pond, Amelia does little strides in the water, going from one end to the other end. Finally, she dips her whole self in and does twirls in the water. The pond is crystal clear when she opens her eyes under water and is relieved, she found her happy place. If she had this memory, she could have other memories. Maybe they're not forever gone. She does a handstand in the pond and sees how long she can hold it. Thirty-one seconds, not too bad. Amelia feeling completely restful, leans her hair back into the water, closes her eyes, and floats on the water. Having her ears in the water, she drains out the birds and sounds on the land. After a while, she opens her eyes and decides to head back to the house. I'll have other days I can come out here. Besides, I'm not sure how long I've been out here, don't want Michael to worry if I'm not back by the time he is. She floats over to her pile of clothes and starts to put them back on. She stops for a moment, noticing one of them is missing. Amelia could have sworn she put on underwear, a black thong. Then again, did she? Having amnesia is really beginning to confuse her. Maybe she had planned to put her underwear on and didn't. Not seeing what else could have happened, she put the rest of her clothes on, ringed out her long hair, and started walking back to the house. I'll take a shower and then put some new clothes on, including underwear this time.

10
Brent

He saw her walking through her house after Michael left. Her face looks cute when she's discovering new things. Is that how she would look when I show her my place? He watches her make a call upstairs. Who's she calling? She doesn't know anyone, did she get a memory back? He sees her turn towards the window and is holding up a card. She must be making a call to a business place. Wondering what it could be, but no way of finding out, he moves on. He could possibly sneak in later to see who the card belongs to. Brent then spots her walking over to the room. Don't go in there, nothing good belongs in there. As she discovers the door is locked, he feels relieved. Even though Michael isn't there, it's better if the room remains a mystery to her.

She leaves, then enters the room to change, with hope in his eyes again, he focuses in on nothing but her. This time she walks in the closet and must have changed in there, because she comes out fully clothed. He curses under his breath again but doesn't stress, those aren't the reasons I love her. There's so much more to her than her body. Brent's heart jumps with so many emotions. He sees her going down the stairs and out the house. His heart pumps faster. She's coming outside, she'll be close to me. I can see her with my own eyes. He's become a professional at this, hiding in the woods. This isn't the first time she's come out here. He thinks of snatching her up this time but goes against that idea. She needs to meet me properly, so she wants me as much as I need her.

As she finally steps into the woods where he's at, she winces and puts a hand on her head. Is she hurt? Looking back up, she has a new look of recognition. This time he knows she remembered something, probably being somewhere so familiar to her. Amelia starts walking a direction she goes often, and Brent slowly follow in his own way. He knows where she's going. It's her favorite place, just like it's his favorite place as well. He gets to see things other people don't. As she first arrives, she eyes the place with a smile. Her eyes are hypnotizing, she could get anything she wants from me. This area has many rocks near the pond, so he always goes to the side where the rocks are low, and everything in the pond is visible. It took Brent a few times until he found the perfect view. At first, she sits there, then she looks around. He ducks his head back behind the tree so not to be seen. Then he feels his body heat as she starts to take off her clothes for skinny dipping. Amelia is facing right towards him, the perfect view. He finally sees her breasts, a thing he's missed watching. His eyes trailing down to the thing only a woman can have, he immediately gets hard for her. She goes into the water slowly, which is better for his viewing. He takes in every inch of her as she slides in the water, her skin getting wet.

Once she is in, he can tell they're both going to be there for a long time. While trying to get more comfortable, he makes a mistake of stepping on a branch, the skinny twig breaks under his weight and makes a sudden sound. Panicking like Amelia, Brent wonders if she saw him. How stupid of me to not check the ground first. What if she saw, should I just come out and grab her now? Should I say I'm one of her neighbors out for a walk? What if she goes and tells Michael what happened? I can't have her do that. He peaks his eyes back out to see what decision he has to make and sees her looking over in the opposite direction of him. Moving his gaze past her, he sees a deer and is relieved it can be blamed on the animal. She didn't see me. Amelia gets lower into the water, but he can still faintly make out her body in the water. She's fully nude and vulnerable. He eyes her clothes and desperately wants something as a souvenir. Wants to smell her again, he knows the perfect piece of clothing for that.

Brent watches her twirl, getting both sights of her in the front and from behind. He switches from one tree to another at the right moments. He's close to the prize. All of a sudden, she does a handstand under water and he sees his opportunity. He bends down, finds the black thong and holds it tight in his hands. Before going back into hiding, he looks at her. The bottom half of her is bare right in front of him. Never has he been this close to her naked body. He reaches out his hand to touch her, then pulls back into reality and moves back to his original tree. She pops her head back up for a breath of air, and Brent sees her front half of her body emerging out of the water. Water dripping off her breasts, everything is glistening in the sun. she raises her hands to push her wet hair back and her body is stretched and exposed. Brent can't take it anymore.

Amelia's Amnesia

He slowly undoes his jeans, takes her newly found underwear and starts pleasing himself. He places her thong to where her most intimate area would connect with his and it makes him that much more excited. As Amelia leans back and floats in the pond, he has full view of her bare body to himself. I can usually only do this at my place just thinking of her. To do it right here, right now in front of her is a sign. We're supposed to be together, I can't wait to feel her not just on the outside, but on the inside as well. His hairline begins to bead up with sweat and he finishes. He loves thinking of how his semen is on her intimate wear. Having nowhere else to put it, Brent places it in his pocket and pulls out his phone. He angles it to have the camera side facing out but hiding the rest behind the tree. He presses record. I'm not creepy for this, she's supposed to be with me right now. This is just to hold me over until my bed is no longer empty. Looking at the screen of his phone, it shows everything he is seeing. Amelia's curves and beauty still wet from being in the water. After about a minute of recording he ends the video, thinking that will be plenty of time whenever he needs to rub one out. This is much better than my imagination, this is the real thing.

She gets out the water and searches through her clothes, he hopes she doesn't wander around looking for her underwear. She pauses and he holds his breathe. After she shakes her head a bit, she continues dressing and walks back towards the house. Breathing again, Brent waits until she is totally out of view. Once she is gone, he doesn't feel satisfied enough from jerking off before. He craves more of her. He strips off his clothes and goes into the pond himself. She was in here, bare skinned, soaking up this water. He sits his phone up on a rock to play the newly done video of her on replay and gets busy once again. Seeing her floating in the water makes him feel like she's actually there with him and it pleases him even more. He lets out a moan this time as he finishes. Being more than satisfied this time. He gets dressed and heads back to his place to put his new souvenir with the rest he has. This will do for now, but he knows he will eventually want more.

11
Michael

He heads back home feeling a bit tired. He doesn't like the city vibe. Doesn't like the city air, it drains him. He has Amelia's pain pills with him. I probably should have gotten it yesterday, but we had much more fun on our date. She seems fine anyways. Michael finally sees their house and pulls into the garage like he does day after day. He sighs at the thought of having to make dinner. Amelia is the one who usually does the woman's work, he's going to fix that tonight. He leaves his car after a moment of silence and walks inside. He sees her sitting in the living room with her white bathrobe on, sipping green tea out of a mug, hair still wet. She took a shower this early?

"Hey babe, what'd you do today?" Pointing at her bathrobe.

"I did what you suggested this morning, I looked through the house and woods. I had a memory come back to me too!" She sits up taller, sounding excited at her discovery.

"Oh yeah? What was it about?" He goes and sits beside her on the couch.

"I have a spot in the woods that I always go to in my free time. You've been there as well, the pond with all the rocks." She sips her hot tea, not taking her eyes from him.

Michael feels concerned that her memory is coming back so soon. It's only been two days. "I'm not sure if it's good for you to be pushing yourself like that?" He sees her frown a bit.

"That's the thing, the memory just came to me. I was scared I wouldn't ever get my memory back. My whole past being a blank slate." Her eyes look worried and lonely.

"Hey, you'll get it back baby. Just don't stress yourself out over it. You have the rest of your life to remember and I'll help you." He kisses her forehead and embraces the back of her neck with his hand. He reassures her with his deep stare, then gets up to start dinner. Spaghetti should be a quick fix. He pulls out the ground beef to thaw for the meatballs and heats a pot up with water.

He heard Amelia in the background. "I almost forgot, the guest bedroom you told me about is locked from the outside, I couldn't get in there. Is there a reason it doesn't lock from the inside like the rest?"

Michael closes his eyes and tilts his head back to take a deeper breath. I shouldn't have given her the idea of going around to explore. "Um, yeah. When the house was being made, the workers accidentally put the doorknob on the wrong way. That's all."

"Oh, well do you have the key? It's about the only room I haven't been in yet." She stands up and walks over to the kitchen with him.

He turns towards her, keeping a calm look even when he feels a bit frustrated. "Honestly, it's nothing to look at. The room is really boring, and we rarely have guests come over. Don't worry about it." After a minute of inspecting his face, her expression turns neutral and nods her head. "Can I help you with dinner? What are you making?"

"Actually, I wanted to talk to you about that."

"About what?"

"Things that need to be done around the house. Before, you used to cook and clean around here. I would appreciate it if you started doing that again since you're here all day and I have to go work." He puts his hand in hers to make the message come across less harsh.

"Um, alright. I guess I can do that. It may take a few days to get used to where things are at." She smiles at him, but it's not a sincere one. She has a bit of doubt written across her face.

"You'll be fine Amelia. You were always good at the house stuff." He gives her a playful wink and she blushes at him. They continue to make the spaghetti together and he feels better that she's around him again. Things will be fine if she stops asking so many questions. He's trying to stay calm, do things right. He hopes she only remembers the good times between them, not the fights they've had. At the moment, the less she knows, the better.

12
Amelia

It's been a few days since she's been back to her regular life and her bruises and cuts are practically gone. The nurse was right, she does heal fast. Ever since the woods, she hasn't had any other memories. Amelia hasn't even been back to the pond, Michael said she should stay in the house more and read some books instead. She's not sure why he feels the need to control her schedule when he's not around, but she decides to listen to keep the peace between them. Lately Michael has been more irritated towards her. Yesterday he yelled for her to come down to the kitchen.

"Hey, what's up?" A bit confused seeing the anger in his eyes.

"What's this?" he points to the kitchen floor.

"Um, I don't see anything." She looks closer at the floor, thinking she missed what he's pointing to.

"The dust on the floor. It's filthy, why is it still there?" He's glaring at her.

"Oh, I'm sorry. I must have forgot –"

"So what, you're going to bring up your amnesia as an excuse."

Amelia blinks in shock. "No, I just forgot. I vacuumed the carpet, wiped down the surfaces, cleaned the dishes, and did the laundry. I thought I got everything."

Michael begins to rub his temples. "Well you didn't get everything. The last thing I want to come home to is a dirty floor that I don't want to step on." He walks over to the closet and grabs a broom with a dustpan. "Fix it." She picks them up and starts sweeping. Did he have a rough day at work? He hasn't acted this way towards me before. At least since I woke up at the hospital. Seeing at how upset he got, she made sure to get every crumb and speck off the floor while he went upstairs to shower.

Today she feels the need to get out. Amelia needs to go somewhere, and not just explore in the woods. She's been in the same place for days and feels a bit suffocated. Michael has also smothered her since she's been back as well. She realizes that's probably because of the accident, but she needs her own space as well. Needs to be around other people. Since the weekend has now approached, she thinks of where she could ask Michael to go. She woke up before him and made sure to get everything in order to avoid what happened yesterday. There, the house is clean. Michael will feel good about this. After cleaning, she began their breakfast. For him, she made scrambled eggs, toast, and bacon. For her, she made sunny side up eggs, a bagel with cream cheese, and some extra bacon she had made. Michael came down the steps, looking at everything to see how good of a job she'd done cleaning. Seeing that all of the cleaning was in fact done, he smiled and gave her a kiss.

"Good morning babe, the house looks great. I told you, you'd be great at this." Seeing that Michael was in a better mood today, she felt more confident about the question she wanted to ask. She doesn't think he would say no to it, but she feels better if he was feeling generous as well. "I made us a few things for breakfast." Michael slightly frowns looking at it.

"On Saturday's you usually make pancakes." At this statement, Amelia feels a little defeated. I'm not trying to mess things up. Seeing her face, he changes his tone.

"Hey, it's okay. This is like our first weekend together. I didn't think about mentioning anything to you, since it was a regular thing for us. Breakfast looks delicious." He gives her a teasing slap on her bottom, and she made a squeaky noise out of surprise. He grabs his plate as she gives him a slap back.

"Aye! Not fair, you have the advantage right now." He turns around and walks backwards into his seat so he's not an open target anymore.

"That's exactly what a person who's losing would say." Amelia sticks her tongue out at him and sits down as well. So far so good. "So…" She picks at her food with a fork. "I see that I have workout clothes in the closet."

"You do." Michael says, seeing where this is going.

"Do you think you could drive me to the gym, so I could get back into that routine?" she bites her bottom lip, anticipating his answer. She needs to go out.

"Of course. You sure you'll be alright there by yourself?" He takes a bite out of his bacon.

"Yeah, I was fine in the woods. I'm sure I'll think of something to do there as well."

Michael thinks for a moment and then says, "Anything you want. If that'll help you then I'm all for it." They both finish up their food, and she begins to get dressed.

Amelia's Amnesia

Amelia finds high waisted spandex and a lime green, sweat resistant, mid drift tank top. She puts her hair up in a high ponytail and wears a pair of running shoes she also found in the closet. Michael comes in. "I put your gym bag in the car, you ready?"

"Yup." She smiles wide and follows him to the car. They don't drive far until they reach the gym they have a membership too. Another memory is inching its way in Amelia's memory. She vaguely recognizes this place. It seems familiar to her. As she gets out of the car and walks into the building, her memory comes back finally. She's been here a lot, not every day, but she would come a couple of times a week.

She walks up to the employees working there and scans her card. Going into the locker room, she finds her usual locker where she puts her stuff. It's in the back corner, and the locker is almost always empty. Amelia comes back out and decides it's a good idea to work on her legs today. She warms up her legs on a treadmill and feels her muscle memory kicking in. she now remembers various workouts she does here. Picking which ones to do, she decides that dead lifts, squats, lunges, and leg lifts are good exercises to start with. Feeling satisfaction of moving around in a new place fills her endorphins and she is moving through things swiftly. Lifting heavy weights and having proper technique. Many men there were either staring or trying to sneak glances her way. She didn't care, she felt more freedom being here. Amelia is halfway into her workout routine when she sees a very familiar person come in the gym. Michael, wearing workout clothes now too, scans his card and waves at her. He sure has been clingy recently, she thinks to herself. At least she got some time to herself before he got there. She waves back and waits for him to come out of the men's locker room.

13
Michael

Michael dropped off Amelia and drove back to the house. He stepped inside and took a look around. Suddenly, he was bored. He's been focused on Amelia this whole time. Even before the accident, they would always be around each other, except for when he had work. Usually whenever she went anywhere, he would drop her off before he went to work. This is our time, we should be together right now. Michael quickly felt betrayal but didn't want it to take over his mood. I said I would do things right this time, I don't want to chase her away again. Instead of anger coming onto him, he decided to get dressed in workout clothes like her and drive back over there.

He puts on grey shorts and a black spandex top. After putting some sneakers on, he grabbed his gym bag and headed to the car. She'll be happy to see me, she probably misses me already. I know I already miss her. Feeling confident in his choice of actions, he thinks of her bright green eyes and starts his car.

Arriving at the gym, he smiles and waves, recognizing Amelia the moment he stepped in. she's the most beautiful woman in there, even without make-up. Amelia smiles and waves back, seeing him as well. I knew she missed me. Going into the locker, he put his gym bag away, and made sure his hair was still neat and slicked back. He hates it when it falls out of place. He likes his hair to be perfect, he likes everything to be perfect. That's one of the reasons he loves Amelia, she's as close to perfect as a fiancée can get. She needs to be my wife already, she'll marry me this time around. No is not an option anymore, I want to be with her for the rest of my life. He walks out and catches up to her.

"Hey babe, what're you doing?" He places his hands around her arms.

"Hey, I was working on my legs today. I'm already halfway done."

"That's fine, I'll skip a warm-up and we can finish it together."

"Okay. Did you come because you were worried about me?" She had a curious look on her face.

"No, I just missed you. This is our time together, you missed me?" He leaned in closer.

"I was having me time." She started to giggle but stopped when Michael frowned. Feeling the sudden tension, she continued by changing the subject. "So, I started doing hip raises, you want to join me." His face lightens and he agrees. Going over to start it, he looks around as she goes first. Several men are poorly sneaking glances at her and how she's moving. One guy beside them isn't shy at looking. Michael glares back and blocks the view the guy had on her. Reading the situation, the random man gets up and moves to another area. Jealousy washes over Michael. This is why we workout together. These pigs can't stop drooling over her. What if one of them takes her? She is my fiancée.

Not noticing a thing, Amelia gets up and smiles at him.

"What?" He says in a bit of a harsh tone. He's wonders how she doesn't see what he sees.

"It's your turn, I finished my first set." She taps his arm, pretending like she's tagging him in. he starts his first round, but is still looking around, feeling extra protective over his prize. The longer they're at the gym, the more upset he begins to feel. It's been sometime since he's had to notice other people besides him appreciate her looks. Many guys love the attention their women get, but I don't. I can't stand it.

"How much longer are we staying here?" He feels impatient.

"I have one more thing I want to do before stretching, why?" Her face looks a bit sad to his tone of voice.

Michael lightens up his tone. "Just wondering, I'm feeling a bit tired. Why don't we go back home and cuddle up to watch a movie?"

"Um, sure. Can I just finish things up first though? I'm almost done, and I feel great!"

"Of course, babe." He kisses her forehead even though it's a little damp from sweat. She smiles and starts walking over to hip abductions. Looking around, Michael catches the same guy looking at her from a far. What a creep. He begins walking over towards him, anger flowing all around him. Who does he think he is? Amelia catching the change of action and stops him.

Amelia's Amnesia

"Hey, why do you look so pissed?"

"This guy won't take his eyes off you. He's a perv." Michael snaps at her.

She looks around. "What guy?"

He looks back to point, but realizes he's gone. Amelia chimes back in. "Maybe it was a person looking at something else. If it's bothering you, we can go. I can find another time to stretch."

"Finally, don't come here again without me. There's too many guys here." Amelia looks down and frowns.

"If it'll make you feel better, I guess we can do that." They get there things together and walk out the gym. I wasn't seeing things, that guy was definitely there, he tries to convince himself. As they go home, she tries to think about what theme of movie they can watch while Michael tries to calm himself. He feels the right to be mad but doesn't want to explode on her. Not like how he used to. They step inside their clean house and he's reminded how dirty and sweaty he is. Following Amelia to the bedroom, she turns to him and smiles. It's not an innocent smile though, she looks seductive to him.

"So I was thinking, since we're engaged, it would only be fair if we started acting a little more like we were." She bats her eye lashes at him. "Why don't we take things from kissing and touching to something a bit more. Want to join me in the shower? You can see how I feel without all these clothes on." She winks at him and his anger disappears. Those guys can look at her all they want. I'm the one who has her heart though. Not needing to say yes, they move to the bathroom where they strip in front of each other and join in the shower for the first time since the hike. He almost forgot how soft and smooth her skin felt. His fingers exploring different holes, making her moan softly in his ear. I'm going to marry her.

14
Brent

Brent sees on his phone that Amelia and Michael are going to the gym. He knows this because he put a tracker in their car. Ever since he found out where she lived and put the tracker under the carpet of their SUV, it's been a lot easier to see what she's up to. Before, he would drive to the coffee shop and sit there for hours, waiting to see if she would come, only having her social media to look at for days.

He sees the direction they're both going, the gym. Quickly, he throws on some workout clothes and a baseball cap to help hide his face in case he needs to. He hurries in his red sedan, excited to see Amelia, and drives to the same gym he signed up at six months ago. When Brent walks in, he's expecting to see the both of them. Michael always insists he goes with her. Instead, it's just Amelia. She's trying to find some alone time again. She frequently does that with Michael when he gets clingy. *She wouldn't do that with me, we would never have a dull moment together.* Seeing that Michael isn't here, Brent moves a bit closer to her. She looks sexy in her outfit. Her mid drift top showing a sneak-peak of her abs and the spandex hugging her body just right. He looks around his surroundings, noticing how many guys check her out as well. It usually does bother him, but what can he do about it? *It doesn't matter, I'm going to be the one to have her, not them.* Brent works out around her and looks at her whenever he gets the chance to.

He respects her love for being fit and healthy. She always tries to better herself and put her best foot forward. Her moves are very precise in each workout, hitting every move perfectly. *No wonder she looks amazing.* About half an hour later, Brent sees her stop what she's doing and waves. He turns his head to see Michael, of course.

He should have known that guy would come. Michael can't be away from her for too long, a reason why he only has one car and made Amelia sell hers when she moved in with him. Convincing her they didn't need two and how it would take up too much space. Michael steps out, and the two of them begin to workout.

This makes things harder for Brent to be close to her. Amelia doesn't worry about people looking at her, but her protective fiancé does. Not wanting to move away from his future wife, Brent stays where he's at. Ever since he got closer to her at the woods, he hasn't wanted to watch her from a far. As he gets mesmerized in the way she moves her hips, Brent sees Michael's glare fixated on him. This isn't good. Never before has Michael or Amelia paid attention to him. Having no idea what to say, he gets up and moves all the way across the gym. Thankfully, Amelia was too focused on her workout to see the tension that was caused over her. I'm starting to slip up, I need to be more careful when he's around.

Brent steps onto a tread mill, being almost out of sight from them. He can barely see Amelia anymore, and aches over it. He feels empty inside, having a distance between him and her. For a year, he's been okay with the space between them, but now it's not enough. He craves more of her. I just need a chance to show her how I'm the one she's supposed to be with. Staying on the treadmill, not wanting to raise anymore alarms, he watches them the rest of the time.

Towards the end, Brent notices how Michael begins to complain about leaving. Who is he to talk to her like that. Every time he sees Amelia be disrespected by Michael, he wants to jump in, but can't. The thought breaks his heart and urges him to get Michael out of the picture. Just then, Michael and he lock eyes again. This time is different, Michael's eyes get dark. Shit. Brent knows that look and what happens following it. As Michael approaches him, he lowers his cap not knowing what to do until Amelia steps in. With this new distraction, Brent seizes him opportunity to get away.

Brent is bigger than Michael but does not want to cause a scene. Does not want Amelia to meet him this way. She helped me, she is the one for me. Fate constantly brings us together. He loves her even more now. I'll get my chance soon, and she'll be all mine.

15
Brent

There he is, with Amelia at the pond. She decides to skinny dip again, her body floating in the water, her hair flowing behind her. Instead of being secretive this time, Brent walks out towards her. He smiles and waves. She smiles back.

"Hey Brent." Joy is in her eyes.

"Hey Amelia, mind if I join you?" He crouches down to reach her at eye level and lifts her chin with his hand.

"I'd love it if you did." She winks at him.

Taking the invite, he strips off his clothes as well and joins her. Wasting no time, they swim towards each other, holding themselves in an embraced hug. She snuggles her head up to his neck and he rests his chin on her head.

"You know this is how things are supposed to be between us?" He turns to look at her.

"I do." She looks up at him.

Both feeling the close touch between each other, then go in for a kiss. Her lips fit perfectly around his, he feels their tongues meet. Brent moves his hands freely around her and she lets him. Departing from their long kiss, she gazes into his eyes and says, "Make love to me." Not needing to respond, Brent leans her up on some smooth rocks and moves in slowly. Just before he makes it in, his alarm clock wakes him up.

Another dream ending too soon. Looking over to the other side of his queen size bed, he's disappointed to see that no one's there, Amelia's not there. He wakes up alone again. His apartments not as big as a house, but it's good enough for him. He doesn't feel claustrophobic in here, not that he has that phobia. It could be big enough for Amelia and him. She wouldn't complain about it. If anything, they would have less space between them. He lives a bit closer to the city than Amelia, but not directly in the city where rent is high. Brent rubs his face before getting up for some coffee, his favorite drink in the morning. He knows it's Amelia's favorite too, always writing her work in a coffee shop. He brews a cup of black coffee. His coffee maker also makes lattes, so Amelia can make her caramel lattes when she moves in with him.

He moves back to his room to look at his calendar. His schedule revolves around her. Brent doesn't have to worry about work getting in the way of that, because he works at home. As a graphic designer, he can be very flexible with his spare time. All of the things he does is for Amelia. He eats healthy for her, works out to look good for her, takes care of his face and skin, uses teeth whitener, and constantly keeps his apartment clean in case she ever wants to go home with him. *You won't have to worry about doing everything for Michael, I'll help you around the apartment with cooking and cleaning. I'm not a child, I know how to clean up after myself.*

He turns to his right to look at the collage he's made. Brent looks at it every morning and night before he goes to sleep. It's a whole collage dedicated to her. Over the past year it's become huge, almost reaching the ceiling and stretching across half the wall. In it are various pictures of her. Some are from her social media pages, others are pictures he's taken. The latest pictures are screenshots from his video of her in the pond. There are other pictures of her at the coffee shop, the gym, walking on the street and sidewalks, watering plants near the windows, and one picture of her sleeping.

Brent got that picture by sneaking into their house one day while she was taking a nap, wanting to have something of hers. After being in the house a few times, he knew how to be quiet and quick. After grabbing a lace bra, he noticed how she was sleeping so peacefully. He pulled out his phone that was on silent and took a photo before leaving. He can't wait until he can watch her sleep in his bed.

Other things Brent added to his collage was her poems. That was the reason he fell in love with her in the first place, it's only right they go up there as well. For a while he was content with just pictures and poems, until he felt like his artwork needed something more to it. That's when he started taking some of her things. Brent knew not to take too much, so Amelia or Michael don't feel alarmed about so many things missing in their home. *It's not wrong of me to take her things, she'll eventually have to move all of her stuff over here.* He looks at the underwear hanging on his wall. He has two bras, one is pink with lace, another is cheetah print with a small gem in the middle of it. Brent also has four different pairs of things of G-strings. The latest thong being the one he used for pleasuring himself in the woods. He goes to smell a purple G-string that was in Amelia's hamper to clean before he took it. Taking in a deep breath, he starts to think of her floral breeze perfume, another thing he loves to smell of her.

Amelia's Amnesia

He bought the same kind she always gets online. He didn't feel right taking that from her, she would have to buy a whole new one. Looking at the bottled perfume on his cabinet, it's halfway full. Brent enjoys spraying it around his apartment and on his pillows, so it feels like she's there when he closes his eyes. Brent's collage is also a gift for Amelia. He wants to show her how much he loves her when she comes over. Not many men would do this for a woman, she will be so grateful that I took the time to make this. It will be a gift she'll never forget.

Smiling about his own thoughts, he gets out his binoculars to see what she's doing around the house today. He needs to see her soon and can't wait much longer. Brent reassures himself that being patient is key. If he moves too fast, then he might lose her. Walking to his car, he settles for what he has right now.

16
Amelia

The weekend is over and it's Monday again. Michael went off to work, so Amelia starts to clean around the house to get it over with. She wonders why the spare room is still locked from the outside, there must be a lot of dust in there by now. Why does he act so weird about it if it's just a spare room? She wants to ask him why he's so sensitive about keeping the room locked from her, but then decides to leave it alone for now. Michael will have to open it up eventually.

    Skipping that room like always, she moves onto watering all the plants. Taking care of the plants makes her want a puppy she can take care of. Why have we never gotten a pet before? Is it something we ever talked about? Finishing all of the daily chores, she moves to the office to choose a book. She chooses a decently sized one in hopes it will last longer and moves back down to the living room. After nine pages in, Amelia hears a knock at the door. That's strange, Michael shouldn't be home for hours? Did someone get lost driving and need directions? If that's the case, I won't be able to help much. She tightens her robe and walks up to the door. Opening it slowly, she sees a guy giving her a huge smile.

    "Hi, can I help you?" She tilts her head to the side.

    "Amelia! Thank God you're okay, I was getting worried about you!" The man immediately goes in for a hug. Okay, so I must have known this guy before.

    "Yeah I'm fine. Are you one of Michael's friends? Don't tell me he sent someone over to check on me." She chuckles and his smile turns to a frown.

    "It's me, Dan." He waits for her to reply, but she's not sure of what to say just yet.

"I'm your friend, Daniel. You haven't responded to any of my texts or calls for two weeks. I came by to see if everything's alright." His eyebrows are arched together, worried.

"Sorry Dan, recently I was in some hiking accident and got amnesia from hitting my head." She lifts her hairline up to show the stitches. "If it makes you feel better, I didn't remember who I was either."

Finally paying more attention to his looks, Amelia studies him. He's not hard to look at, in fact, he's very attractive. He's about four inches taller than her. Unlike Michael's hair, Dan lets his dark brown hair loose. It flips in all directions, just barely reaching his eyebrows. He has a tan, showing that he's been outside in the sun a lot. His light blue eyes are stunning. Dan has facial stub that he clearly grooms and maintains around his sharp jawline. His lips are thin compared to hers, and his nose has a soft natural touch to it that fits him right.

Amelia then looks down his tall body. He is very muscular. She assumes he must have a physical type of job. He's wearing a green t-shirt that shows the mass of his pecs and abs. Some dark brown hair shows on his arms, that are big enough to lift her with ease. Having on khaki shorts, she can see his calves toned and fitting the rest of his body structure. Amelia can't help but admire the man she's staring at. Then she realizes his concern of what she just told him.

"Wait what? You were hurt?" He brushes back her hair to look at the one cut that's still trying to heal. "Did someone do this to you? You shouldn't go hiking alone."

"I wasn't, I was with Michael."

"He did this to you! What time is he getting back, I'm going to have a talk with him."

"No, no!" Amelia rushes to reassure him. "Michael went off the trail to use the restroom when it happened. No one else was on the trail, they said I tripped and fell. My head hit a tree."

"That must have been a lot for you." He says with empathy. He walks closer to hug her in a strong embrace, her head on his chest.

"It's okay, really. I'm still trying to remember things." She smiles up at him.

"Is that why you haven't been on your phone?" He brushes his fingers through her hair, comforting her.

"No, I actually lost it while falling. The detectives haven't found it. I wasn't trying to ignore you, sorry to get you all worried." Her smile turns to a small frown.

"You have no reason to apologize. I'm just glad you're okay. Has Michael given you a new phone yet, I can put my number in it." He leans back and looks at her.

"No, he said he would, but hasn't brought it up since. Michael actually told me that I didn't really have any friends in New York, why wouldn't he mention you?"

Amelia's Amnesia

Dan rolls his eyes. "He doesn't like me. Said you were lying about us just being friends. You stopped mentioning me to him, because it always ended in fights." His eyes gets sad. "How has he been treating you?"

"Not bad, I have noticed his short temper when it comes to certain things, but that's it." Amelia sometimes wonders if Michael is the right fit for her. There must have been something special about him if I said yes when he proposed.

Dan continues their conversation. "So, you don't remember anything?"

"Well I had two memories. One was when I was in the woods, and the other was at the gym. I called a shrink to help me out, but I'm not quite sure how I'm going to get there. I didn't tell Michael I was going, because he wants me to take things slow and we only have one car."

Dan sticks his hands out. "I'll drive you. I'll even be there for support. Then you won't have anything to worry about."

"Um, you sure? It's in two days, in the afternoon. Don't you have work?"

"I actually don't on Wednesday, this is perfect! I'm taking you." He taps her on the shoulder. "Do you have the shrink's card? Let me see it."

Amelia jogs up to the office and takes the card that hasn't been touched in nearly a week. She comes back to him walking around the living room and hands it to him.

"Great, we'll go together. So you've been here alone?"

"Yeah, it's been kind of boring."

Dan thinks for a moment. "Want to go to the pond? I got some swim trunks in the car. We can hang out like we used to and catch up on things?"

She stops to consider this. She realizes she needs to get her old life back and agrees. Amelia goes back up to change in a normal turquoise colored bikini and wore a sundress to cover some more skin.

As they walked through the path, he knew exactly where they were going, they must have hung out here before. Feeling more relaxed around someone who seems caring, they both step into the pond. Dan did not seem to be a perv when she took off her dress, which meant they were truly friends, like he said.

Amelia and Dan stay in the pond for awhile and talk about each other. She finds out he's a construction worker, who's 26 years old. He told her that they first met at the grocery store a year and a half ago. He made a corny food joke that made her laugh, and they stayed as friends. That was back when she still had her own car. Since then, they usually text and meet up at places to say hi. In the pond, they played Marco, Pollo and tested to see who could stay in a hand stand underwater longer. She won that contest and wasn't shy to brag about it.

Checking his phone, he looks back at her. "We should probably head back now, I should go before Michael gets home. I'll be back over in two days to take you to Dr. Mart's office." He holds out his hand to help her out of the water. They get back and hug each other goodbye.

Amelia takes a shower and blow dries her hair, so it doesn't look wet to Michael. She has some questions for him and doesn't want him to begin questioning her when he first walks in the house. She reads her book until she hears his car pull into the garage.

17
Michael

He steps inside to see Amelia reading again. He's glad she took his advice, she doesn't need to waste so much time in the woods. She has things she has to get done here. Michael walks over and kisses her on the cheek.

"Hey babe, what are you making for dinner tonight?" He loosens his tie.

"I was thinking of making salmon with steamed vegetables." Amelia puts her book on the short table in the living room.

"That sounds good." He sits on the couch and pulls Amelia onto his lap. She rests there with her hand tracing a circle on his chest.

"I actually had a question to ask you." She's not looking at him.

What could she be asking me? "What's up?"

"I was wondering when I could get a phone since my other one is gone. I remember you mentioning how you would help me with that. It could help me communicate with you while you're out working." Her eyes meet his when she is done talking.

He let's out a sigh. "It hasn't even been a week yet, we've both been busy. I'll get to it, but you've got to stop rushing things."

Amelia begins to look frustrated. "Why is it that you have a car, phone, and job, but I can't have anything? You want to even control what I do while you're not here."

He scoffs at her remark. Is she really arguing with me right now? "Control? I'm only giving you good advice and saying what you should be doing. You don't need those things, be happy with what you have."

"Be happy? I feel trapped. What happened to my friends or the people I know?" She gets off his lap at this point.

She is so ungrateful for what I've given her. "Stop complaining about the life I've given you. Many women would be lucky to be in your position. I told you, you don't have friends around here, it's just us."

"I know you're lying. Why are you hiding things from me? What's really in that room, it doesn't seem to be a guest room if it has to be constantly locked." She's standing up, clearly upset.

"Stop asking me about that room! If I say it's nothing, then it's nothing!" He get's up and gets right up in her face. Her reaction is to back up until her back meets the wall. He puts his hand on the wall, next to her face. His face shows anger all around it. "Don't ever question me again, this is ridiculous! I'm helping you, just listen and go with it!"

Amelia says nothing, her whole body looks terrified. Now she really feels trapped. He pauses to take a few deep breaths, still keeping her at the wall. I can't do this, she'll try to leave again, I don't want that. He tries to calm his voice. "So we both got heated just now. Why don't I go upstairs to take a shower and you can start dinner for us. We can settle down and start tonight over."

She still doesn't talk but nods instead. He takes his hand off the wall and heads for the stairs. He looks back to make sure she doesn't try to leave, even though she can't. He has the car keys, not her. This will be better in the morning. She needs to learn how to be appreciative. She looks back at Michael and walks over to the kitchen, prepping the meal.

He steps into the shower and leans his head down, exhausted from today. He needs to learn how to control his temper. I said I would do things differently this time. If I want a wife and kids, I need to do things right. Michael lets the water hit his back for a few more minutes before he turns the shower off. He's going to walk down a whole new person, she'll overlook that argument in no time.

18
Amelia

Ever since Monday, Amelia has seriously reconsidered her relationship. The outburst he had is not something she wants in a relationship. Why was he so mad about me having simple things, like a phone? Why was he so mad about the guest room? Her curiosity for that room has grown, but not knowing how to open the door, her curiosity will have to wait. Will he ever open the door? She almost doesn't want him to, scared about what she might see.

Amelia stops dozing off and begins to get ready for when Dan comes over. It's Wednesday and she hopes he's still going to take her to see Dr. Mart. She really needs this. Even though she's had a couple of memories, she desperately wants more. Her life of who she was before this is completely blank, only having two different people trying to guide her. Michael doesn't want her to push things, but maybe that's what she needs. She parts her hair to the side like usual and lets the waves in her hair fall down around her. She uses brown and beige eyeshadow to have a natural shade around her eyes and applies mascara to make her eye lashes stand out. Next, she lightly adds some pink lipstick and some blush on her cheek bones. She decides to wear a tan blouse with regular blue jeans. She finds a tan pair of sandals that matches her outfit and feels ready to go.

Amelia waits for about five minutes downstairs until she hears Dan's car engine pull up. Not wasting any time, she leaves the house and gets in his car. With a one arm hug, she greets him. "Thanks for coming. I was nervous you might have forgotten." She buckles her seatbelt.

"I would not forget this. You made my day off a little more exciting anyways." He playfully smiles at her and puts his car in reverse.

He drives her out to the city, where Dr. Mart is supposed to be. She looks at the small brick building. She suddenly feels anxious to actually take the first step by going in. Dan must have noticed her change in emotion. "Everything will be fine. I'll go in with you and sit in the waiting room until you come out."

Amelia faces him. "Thanks, I guess we should go in before I'm late." She gives a nervous giggle and gets out of his car. As they cross the street, his hand is on her upper back for support. She opens the door and walks in to meet a receptionist.

"Hi, do you have an appointment with Dr. Mart?" The lady asks her. She is a young woman in her 20's with short, platinum hair and red lips.

"Yes, my name is Amelia Jones."

The lady looks at the computer screen. "Ah yes, Ms. Jones. If you take a seat I'll let him know you're here." She smiles and points to a row of cushioned seats.

"Thank you." Amelia smiles back and then goes to sit down next to Dan. She still feels nervous, but hopeful. She needs this.

A few minutes later, a man walks out into a waiting room. Dr. Mart does not look how Amelia pictured him to be. She imagined he would be an old man, with gray hair and glasses. Instead, he looks to be in his 40's, slim, with a full head of orange hair. His skin is pale like her's, and he has hooded shaped hazel eyes. Since Dan and her are the only people in the room, his gaze falls on them. "Hi, you must be Ms. Jones." He walks towards her.

She gets up from her seat. "I am." He reaches his hand out and she shakes it formally. Dr. Mart then turns his head slightly over to Dan. "And you are?"

"I'm Dan." He's next to shake his hand. "I'm her friend, I also gave her a ride here." He nods, then turns back to Amelia. "Are you ready?"

She lets out a breath of air. "Yes." They both go into a back room.

In the room, there is a blue sofa on her end, and a regular cushioned chair on his end. "Please have a seat." His hand gestures over to the sofa. She walks over and smells the scent of lavender all over the room. It helps her stay calm. "Shall we start?" He's in his seat as well now. "Sure." Amelia clasps her hands together on her lap.

He looks at his notebook and reviews something from it as he speaks to her. "The hospital informed me about what happened recently and I'm glad you took their advice in coming." He looks at her and continues. "Do you know Dan? The only person reported to be at the hospital with you was Michael."

She crosses her leg. "To be honest, I don't remember anyone right now. He came by Michael and I's house wondering if I was okay, because I hadn't responded to him in a while. It seemed like he really knew me, and it was comfortable to be around him."

Amelia's Amnesia

Dr. Mart tilts his head slightly. "Why would he have a reason to be concerned?"

"He doesn't totally trust Michael to be a good guy. Apparently they have different views of each other."

He begins writing in his notepad. "How do you feel Michael has been?"

She looks at the beige wall to think. "He can be good and patient with me, but there are other times when he's not. I'm still not sure how he was before the accident. Now, he has a short temper. It seems like he needs to be in control, but sometimes I wonder if that's just because of what recently happened."

Dr. Mart looks back up at her. "It might be ideal to observe his behavior a bit deeper and to make a conclusion from there if it's normal for him or not. Would you feel comfortable asking him why his behavior has been like that?"

She begins playing with one of her fingers. "I'm not sure, our last argument was uncomfortable. I could observe him more like you said."

His eyebrows arch in. "What did he do that made you uncomfortable?"

"He kind of trapped me against a wall towards the end of it. That's when I stopped arguing with Michael and he moved on."

"If you ever feel uncomfortable with him again, please give me a call." He looks at her and writes again in his notepad. "For today's session, I do want to help you remember a little bit. I went online and printed off some pictures of the trail that you and Michael had been on the day you had the accident." He bends over some to pick up some pictures. "Hopefully if you look back at where you were at, your memory will show us something."

"Okay, I want to try anything." Amelia moves to the edge of her seat, ready to take a closer look at what he has.

Dr. Mart shows some pictures of the trail. She studies them closely. He lets her look at them for a long time before flipping to the next. The images are various angles of the dirt trail. He flips to the part where the path goes up towards a hill and it seems familiar. She squints her eyes and tries to focus. Not saying anything, Dr. Mart holds the picture there, seeing the change in her face. Her brain goes into overdrive and her head is slowly forming what it's trying to re-create. She was on the trail, except she wasn't alone. There's a person there as well, but it's a blank figure. She tries to focus even more, no longer looking at Dr. Mart's image, but looking at what's playing in her head.

"Amelia, tell me what's happening."

"I'm remembering something, I'm on the trail."

"What else is going on?"

She keeps thinking, not sure of what to say yet. She feels frightened like she did on the path. Her and the figure are going back and forth about something, the tension begins getting intense. The blank person moves closer to her, so she back up. The mysterious person is moving their arms a lot, and then it happens. There's a push and then nothing else after that. Amelia gasps at the sudden shift of things. It wasn't an accident. Someone was there, and they pushed me. I never tripped and fell, I wasn't alone on the trail.

Dr. Mart is no longer holding the pictures. "What happened."

She feels panicked, unsafe. Amelia's looking towards the floor to make sense of what she just saw. Someone tried to hurt her. Maybe they're still trying to hurt her. Is she safe? She has no idea who to be looking for, that's something her brain left out.

Her nerves get the best of her and she jumps up from her chair, not being able to sit any longer. Dr. Mart puts his hands up and asks her to have a seat. Not paying any attention to him, she walks out the door, wanting to leave the room. She goes back to the waiting room where Dan is still sitting in the same chair, reading a magazine. He looks up surprised to see her out so soon. He opens his mouth to say something, but she speaks first. "I need to go."

Looking at her expression, he nods. "Okay, I know a place we can go and sit down for a bit."

Before the receptionist can intervene, she walks through the doors and towards Dan's car. She can't be in there anymore. It was too much at once for her to handle. What she's been told isn't true. What people think isn't true. She needs to sort things out and figure out who that person is. Dan catches up to her and they get in the car. Not saying anything, he starts his car and they drive in silence.

19
Amelia

They pull up to a small coffee shop. She wonders why Dan chose this place but knows he must have a good reason to.

"We're here." Breaking the silence, he looks at her.

"What made you think of this place?" She now turns to him.

"It's a familiar place for you. Thought it might help."

They both step out of the car and head inside. As soon as Amelia is in, the smell becomes familiar to her. There's a sense of comfort in this little coffee shop. Looking around, she begins to remember everything about it. "I've been here before. I've been here a lot, how did you know?"

"You've told me about this place. Sometimes we used to meet up here to talk and catch up with each other." Relaxing his shoulders in the warm environment, he walks over to get in line. Amelia follows as she looks up at their menu board. Recognizing the caramel latte as her favorite, she smiles about having a piece of her past back. The smile soon fades as she remembers what other memory she regained. Someone actually tried to hurt her two weeks ago. Not wanting to panic again, she shakes off the memory and looks at the baked goods they offer as well.

They reach the front of the line where Dan orders first. He asks for a regular cappuccino and a slice of blue berry pie. Amelia gets her normal caramel latte and added a banana nutmeg muffin. She didn't realize how hungry she felt until now. After receiving their orders, they find a free table and sit down.

"I had a memory." She starts their conversation first.

"Well that's great! Why did you seem in a rush to get out of there then?"

"It was a memory of someone pushing me down the hill. On the trail Michael and I was on."

"Wait what? So it wasn't an accident, who did it?" Dan puts down his fork and gives his full attention towards her.

"I don't know, it was too faded for me to see."

"Well you got to tell the police. That person might still be out there." He's already pulling out his cell phone.

Amelia reaches her hand over to lower his phone down. "I will, trust me. I just want to remember who it was first, so they have something more to go off of then just a blurry memory."

He looks at her face before sighing in defeat. "Thank you for at least telling me. Someone has to know in case something else happens. You know I'm going to be coming by more to check on you right?" They both laugh and she feels a little bit better having Dan as company again.

He starts another conversation with her. "Are you going to tell Michael about this?"

Amelia frowns, she's not sure of how he's going to react. "I don't know. The last argument we had wasn't fun and you said he definitely doesn't like you."

"You guys are arguing already? Tell me if it gets too out of hand again, you can come stay with me." Dan takes a bite out of his pie.

"So this is a normal thing Michael does? Also, you don't need to offer your place. I'll figure something out if I need to leave."

Dan shakes his head and waves his fork in the air. "Nope, I insist you consider coming over for any reasons. I don't have a house, but I do have a spacious apartment. I'll make an extra room your bedroom if need be. Besides, you're a ball of fun to be around, you would be doing me a favor." She laughs and slaps his arm.

"Have you ever seen Michael and I argue?" Amelia sips her latte.

"Not in person, but you'll talk about it sometimes. At one point you were considering leaving."

What? Michael never told me that. The whole time he made it seem like we were a happy couple planning on having kids. Do I even know who Michael truly is? "Did I actually leave him?"

"No, at least you didn't tell me if you did. I never thought he was too good for you, but I wanted you to make that decision for yourself." Dan then adds. "Again, my place is open if you need somewhere to go. I don't want you to feel like you're stuck at his house."

"Thanks, I might actually consider that if things get worse." She looks at her half-eaten muffin. "What if someone is stalking me? I'm not sure if it may have been a random person who pushed me, or someone who followed me there?"

Amelia's Amnesia

"Jeez, I guess that could be possible. Do you know anyone who would do that?"

"No, I don't remember anyone." She frowns, feeling like she's stuck at a dead end.

"Right, I guess that was a stupid question for me to ask. You never mentioned anything like that to me before, so that doesn't answer much either." He can see the mix of emotions she's feeling right now. "Hey, I don't want you to worry too much. I'll check on you frequently and get my place ready in case you need to suddenly go. Once we figure out what really happened, we will both go to the police station and have them take it from there."

"Thank you Dan, I'm glad I have someone like you around." She looks at his blue eyes and feels safe again. He looks into her green eyes and leans over their small table. He runs his fingers through her black hair and pulls her gently in for a kiss. His kiss is soft, careful, Amelia feels shocked, not expecting this at all. After a few seconds of being interlocked with each other, she pulls away, not sure of what to say. "Um."

Dan face turns a light red out of embarrassment. "Wow, that was out of line. I'm really sorry Amelia."

"Michael and I aren't perfect, but that doesn't mean I should run off to you." She gets defensive.

"I know! And that's not why I offered my place. I'm not sure why I just decided to do that. We've never done that before, I'm sorry." His words come out in a fast ramble.

"I need to go home, please."

"Of course, I'll take you back." He looks down at the table.

They get into his car and drive off, both not talking. Amelia's head is flooded with thoughts. She feels confused about what just happened, but also didn't mind the way his lips felt on hers. Feeling guilty at that thought as well. I'm with someone, I can't have any feelings for someone else. Maybe this was why Michael didn't like us being friends? But then Dan said we have never done this before?

They arrive back at Michael's house. The lights are on, which must mean he's already home.

"Drop me off here, I'll walk the rest of the way." Worry fills her as she wonders what will happen inside.

"Okay, I hope we can get past what happened today." He looks hurt.

Not saying anything back, Amelia closes the door and walks to the front of the house. Thinking about how bad this is going to look. She's stands still for a moment before opening the door. She needs to be careful of what she says.

20

Brent

He's watching Amelia getting ready. On his calendar, Brent wrote down Amelia's appointment with the shrink today. He overheard Dan and her talking about it. Brent actually doesn't mind Dan, he's a good friend to her. A lot better than Michael, he's the problem. Dan is just trying to make sure she's okay and getting the help she needs. Dan should be there soon, so Brent decides to get ready himself to drive to the city.

As Dan and Amelia arrive, he's there too. He's careful to keep his distance. Brent wonders what the shrink and her will talk about, what she'll remember. He tries to keep calm while she's inside there, anxious for her to come back out. Not too long after, Brent sees her come out and walk over to Dan. She seems stressed and on the verge of having a panic attack. He wishes he could cuddle her in his arms all day, but he can't. Dan and Amelia leave the building soon after, so Brent starts his car, ready to leave as well.

He sees Dan drive to the local coffee shop that Amelia loved to go to. It's probably to comfort her. That's what Brent would do for her. He gets out of his car and goes in with them. He needs to find out what happened during her therapy session and why she cut it short. Brent knows that whatever he hears, it can't be good. As they're in line, Brent overhears Amelia remember this place. At least there's some happiness in her day. He's glad she's at her favorite place again, the place he first saw her. Although Brent is broken up about how she feels right now, she looks kind of cute when she's scared.

They all sit down, Brent still trying to stay hidden as usual. Amelia tells Dan how she saw someone push her on the trail. Brent holds his breath for a moment, does she know now what happened? When she tells Dan the memory was too blurry, he breaths again. He knows the day she finds out about what happened on the trail, it will be a big mess, but he can worry about that another day. She also mentions how things haven't been going well between her and Michael. Brent knows this, he gets furious when he sees how Michael treats her. She's a beautiful prize that deserves better. Amelia deserves me, and I deserve her. Dan would like Brent as her boyfriend. Brent would treat her like a queen.

Then it happens, Dan kisses Amelia. Maybe he can't trust Dan like he thought he could. Blind sighted, he holds back the jealousy. Will Dan have to be a problem that I have to fix as well? Brent sees Amelia reject him and he feels a bit more at ease. Dan is just a friend, and that's all he will be to her. Brent leaves, knowing there's nothing more to see there.

Brent will be her number one man. Dan and Michael aren't going to stop him. Brent will meet her soon, he can feel it.

21
Michael

She isn't in the house when he gets back. Michael wonders if she snuck off to the woods, she isn't supposed to be there. He told her to stay home and read books from now on. Michael looks around the place, at least she watered the plants and cleaned the place up. Still, it's not acceptable that she snuck off. How can I trust her as my wife if she does that? I'm going to have to put a tighter leash on her. He heard a car stop, then drive away. Not many cars come through here. Michael waits as he hears the front door open slowly, it's Amelia. This is worse than the woods, what was she doing without me? She won't look at him.

"Where have you been?" He crosses his arms, impatient.

"I went to the city." She's still looking down.

"Went to the city? With who, because you don't have a phone to get an Uber." She pauses before she answers. "Dan took me."

He was at a loss for words. She went out with a man, a man he told her to stop seeing. How did she know about Dan? Michael becomes furious, he's losing his grip on her. "Why are you seeing him! I told you not to ever see him again. Why is another man giving you a ride, or even at my house?"

"He was checking on me, he said I had not replied to him in a while and got worried."

"So you've been talking to him as well?"

She fumbles with her words. "I don't remember what I used to do. Dan said we were only friends and nothing else."

"Yeah, that's what a guy is going to tell you Amelia. Why did you go on a date with him in the city then?"

"It wasn't a date, I had a therapy appointment with the shrink. He offered to take me when he came by to check on me."

Michael's face starts to feel hot, his voice getting louder after each sentence. "Didn't I say not to go to therapy. Do you choose not to listen or am I not making myself clear?"

Amelia tries to explain herself. "I just wanted to remember my past again. I saw someone push me on the trail as well. I didn't trip and fall."

"Wait what? No one was there, what did that shrink do to you?"

"No, I remembered it. I just couldn't see who the person was."

"Yeah, probably because the shrink wanted you to think that so you would go back. There was nobody on the trail, I checked."

Amelia goes to say something, but then is uncertain of what to say. They're both standing there, saying nothing to each other. Michael tries to process everything. She called a phony shrink behind his back, and then asked a 'friend' to take her there when he wouldn't be home.

"Don't worry about dinner tonight, you won't have any." He says in a sudden calm voice.

"What? You're not even going to let me eat now?" She looks at him like he's crazy.

"Yes, you need to think about what you did." Michael walks over and grabs her arm firmly. He pulls her up the stairs and into their room, not caring if she tries to resist. He tosses her toward the bed. "I'll be waiting for an apology when I get back up." He shuts the door before she can respond.

Going back downstairs he thinks about what he's going to make for dinner tonight. I handled that a lot better than how I used to. He still needs to figure out how he's going to stop this from happening again. She can't embarrass him like that again. Walking around the city with someone else. He's not going to give her a chance to do that again.

22
Michael

After Amelia apologized to him last night, he felt better. He got some control back in his house. That's not enough for him though. Michael doesn't want this to happen again, he needs to make more rules for her. As he gets up to take a shower, she goes to the kitchen to start breakfast. So far the morning is going well. While in the shower, Michael thinks of what he's going to do. A few ideas pop into his head and he chooses which ones are the best. He wonders if he should open up the spare room again, but quickly decides against it. I said I would do better this time, I'm not going to open up that room again. She would definitely leave if I used it. Making up his mind, Michael turns off the shower and gets dressed before heading downstairs.

He comes down to scrambled eggs, bacon, and mixed fruit. Amelia doesn't say anything. He takes a few bites before talking to her.

"So there's going to be some changes."

Amelia looks at him finally. "What changes."

"I can't trust you, so I'm changing a few things. First, you will not be leaving this house anymore. You are to stay here unless we're about to go to the gym. The woods don't count either, you need to stay inside. This is my house, so you will follow my rules."

"That's a little much, don't you think. I need some sun once in a while."

He puts his finger up for her to hold on. "I'm not done yet. In two days, on Saturday, I'm having cameras installed in the house as well. This is so I know what's going on and I can see if you are in here." Amelia's mouth drops open in disbelief. Michael continues. "You are not to talk to the handymen who come to install them. You've talked to enough men."

"Dan was the only person I talked to."

"Yes, and that's one too many. This is final. If you didn't want this to happen, maybe you should have thought about the consequences first. I'm scheduling it at work." He continues his last decision. "I am also going to get rid of our landline before going to work. I can't have you calling whoever you want. I will not be getting you a cell phone either, not until you earn it."

Her mouth is still gaped open. "You can't treat me like I'm some pet, I'm a person. Yes, I should have told you what was going on and I didn't, because of how mad you've been lately, but you can't lock me up in a house. I'm not a locked away princess."

"Well, you are now." He finishes his last bite, kisses her on the forehead, and goes to throw out the landline. He has the power again. This will work, she'll get used to this. Michael thinks of how much he gives her. She lives in a beautiful house, she shouldn't want to leave. Her fiancé is handsome as well and successful. I take care of her. She will see that eventually, she's lucky.

Michael gets in his car with the unplugged landline. He plans to through it in a dumpster near work, where she can't go get it. On his way to work, he makes his appointment to set up cameras in his house. He asks that they set up cameras in all the rooms, except for one, the locked room.

He walks into work with a smile on his face. Amelia's not going to wear the pants in this relationship, that's for the men. Feeling his ego grow, he winks at the receptionist and goes into his office. He has a surgery today and some consultations. Getting focused, he plans to have a good day.

23

Amelia

She is still shocked with what just happened. Michael took things way too far. She can't contact anyone and will soon have no privacy. Amelia can't imagine being inside all of the time, not even being able to walk outside the house. She thinks of how she can get out by Saturday, before things get worse. If only he didn't take the landline, then she could have called Dr. Mart to tell him what's happened.

Amelia remembers what Dan suggested. If things got bad, she could move in with him for some time. At first she felt happy to have a way out, but now she's not so sure. Ever since he kissed her, she's had mixed feelings. It was completely unexpected, and she's engaged. Her engagement is about to be over, but it still felt weird being kissed by another man. Maybe if she wasn't with Michael, Amelia could see herself with Dan. He treats her well and they had so much fun the day they hung out at the pond. It's not like he was a bad kisser, it just happened at a bad time. Why haven't Dan and I considered dating before? Was it because Michael was in the picture the whole time? Or has she just only seen him as a friend until now?

Shaking that thought out of her head, she thinks of any other options. Maybe if she looks around the house, she may find something. Just as she finished the dishes, Amelia hears a knock at the door. She wasn't expecting anyone. Michael should be at work and the workers shouldn't be here until Saturday. Could it be Dan? She didn't think he would come back after the awkward moment they had yesterday. She walks to the front, still in her robe, and opens the door. It is Dan. She looks at him, but he looks at the floor.

"Hey, I had a lunch break so I came to check on you."

She pulls him inside. "Michael has gone crazy."

Dan now looks up at her face, concerned. "What did he do?"

"He took the landline out of the house so I can't make calls. I am no longer supposed to leave the house, including just outside the house, and to make sure I follow his rules, he's putting cameras all around the house Saturday."

"He's going to keep you in the house with nowhere to go and no one to call?"

She runs her fingers through her hair, feeling the stress creep inside her. "I don't know what to do. I don't have a choice over anything, I don't remember anyone, and I apparently quit my job to stay here with Michael."

Dan looks puzzled. "What? You never quit writing poetry, did he tell you that?"

"Yeah, he said I quit to plan the wedding and for when we had kids." She shudders at the thought. This is a nightmare, Michael cut off anything she used to have.

"Hey, I am still sorry about what happened yesterday, but you are still welcome at my place. Not because I want anything sexual from you, but because I'm worried about your safety here and you're my friend."

She pauses to really consider this. Does she really have a choice? If she doesn't go with Dan, Michael will keep her locked away from the world. Amelia thinks of which place is worse and doesn't hesitate on her decision. "Okay, I need to get out of here."

"Great, we can go today." He puts his hands out, emphasizing his suggestion.

"I don't have anything packed though and I'm not sure what I should pack in this situation." She looks around.

"Here's what we can do. Spend today looking for what you want to take. I'll take off work tomorrow to come over to pick you up. By then, you'll know what to take with you. You should pack lightly so we don't have to make any trips back."

Amelia ponders the thought for a second. It actually sounds like a good plan. The best one so far. "Yeah, let's do it. I'll pack after Michael goes to work and wait for you here. I probably won't have a whole lot to pack since I don't remember the things I usually would." She lets out a small laugh at her joke. Dan smiles and gives her a hug.

"I got to get back to work now. I'll come back tomorrow, have everything ready so we can go. This won't work if we try it after the cameras are installed."

"Got it, I'll see you tomorrow." They hug one last time and he leaves, brushing the flips of brown hair away from his forehead. She smiles as his hair falls right back where it was before. He's very different than Michael, not needing everything to be perfect or in order. Amelia once again wonders what it would be like to be with a guy like him, but then shrugs the thought away. We're just friends, that's it.

She goes up to the bedroom and searches through things she might need. This plan has to work. She can't deal with Michael much longer and Friday is her only chance to become free.

24

Amelia

She wakes up in the morning, today is the big day. Amelia feels nervous, but excited to leave this place for good. Realizing Michael is laying right next to her, she covers her emotions. She can't have him suspect anything. He needs to go to work like it's a normal day. Amelia faces away from him as she gets out of bed to walk out of the room.

"Hey, wait."

She freezes, what is he going to say.

"You're in a hurry. Didn't say good morning or anything."

Amelia turns around with a smile. "Good morning, how did you sleep?"

"I slept fine, what about you?" He arches an eyebrow at her.

She barely slept at all. "I got a lot of sleep." Without adding anything else, she turned around and went down the steps.

In the kitchen, she wonders if he caught onto anything. She hears the shower start, that's a good sign. He's not doing anything out of the ordinary. I really need to calm down before he decides to skip work today. She starts making breakfast for the both of them, the last one she'll make for him. Michael comes down as she's finishing up. Amelia avoids making eye contact with him. She doesn't want her eyes to tell him what's wrong.

He finishes getting ready for work and is about to leave. She can feel the rush bubbling inside of her. He turns to her before he opens the door. "Remember, the cameras are getting installed tomorrow. Don't talk to the guys who put them in. I'll be here as well."

"Okay, I won't do anything." Because I won't be here.

Michael kisses her forehead before going out the door. When she hears the SUV fade away down the road, she starts to pack. In the bedroom closet, she pulls out a small suitcase she found. Amelia packs a few pieces of clothing, shirts, pants, shoes, and underwear. Next, she goes into the bathroom and packs some make-up, hairbrush, shampoo, conditioner, tooth paste, and her tooth brush. She looks around the room and realizes she doesn't have anything else to pack. Dan told her to pack light. She was frantic to get ready to leave but didn't realize it would only take a few minutes. Looking at the clock, she has a few hours of free time.

Looking around the hallway, her eyes land on the guest bedroom. The whole time she's been here, he never opened it up to her. What is he hiding in there? Seeing that this is her last chance to find out, she tries to open it. Pulling hard, the doorknob doesn't budge. She sighs in frustration. There's something important behind that door, I just know it.

Amelia thinks in front of the door. If it locks from the outside, there must be a key. She walks to the bedroom and starts searching. She goes through all of his stuff but finds nothing. She thinks of other places Michael would put it and thinks of his office. That would make sense. She walks in and starts looking around the bookshelf, nothing. She turns and looks at the desk. She sits in the chair and searches around the surface of the desk. There's barely anything on there still. She turns her attention to the drawers. Last time she was in here, Amelia didn't open them in case they were private. She opens the top right one and sees a silver key on top of some papers. Yes!

She grabs the key, it looks like the right size for the doorknob. She rushes out of the office and to the guest room door. She slowly puts it in, making sure it does fit instead of jam, and turns the key until she hears a click. The door is unlocked. Feeling excited about what she's about to see, she opens the door immediately. Squinting inside, Amelia can't see anything. The room is so dark. Moving her hand around the wall, she touches a light switch and flips it on. She jumps back at what she sees. It's not a guest room at all.

The whole room is black, including the floor. There's no window in here to let in sunlight like the other rooms. There's no bed either. The only thing is a chain hooked up to the wall. It comes back to her. What this place really is. Michael's time-out room. This memory comes with a flashback. A few months after Amelia moved in with Michael and sold her car, they were getting into more fights. One day he snapped, she sees the conversation.

"I'm not your personal maid, the house won't always be absolutely perfect!"

Michael is yelling back. "If you're going to be my wife, then it does have to be perfect! Now do it again!" His face is getting red.

Amelia's Amnesia

"Then I guess I won't be your wife! Find someone else to do all this work." She goes to leave, but he grabs her.

She looks at him and his eyes turn dark. "You need some time to think about what you did wrong."

"Excuse me! What I did wrong?" Amelia looks at him like he's a different person.

"Yes, you need a time-out."

She lets out a sarcastic laugh. "Time-out, I'm not five years old. I'm a grown woman."

Michael yanks her arm and drags her up the stairs and opens a new room he just renovated. He turns on the light and continues to pull her in. Amelia is thrown to the floor and has a chain locked around her ankle in no time. She is terrified. He flashes a key in front of her face. "I'll give you some time to think and will come back for your apology."

He gets up to leave. She tries to run to him, to reach for the key, but falls when the chain runs out of length. Holding her ankle, he shuts the door on her and it's completely dark. As she stayed in there, she couldn't tell if it was day or night, but she had been in there a while. Her stomach hurts with hunger and her lips go dry. Michael finally comes in.

"Did you learn your lesson?"

She nods, too thirsty to talk. He un-does her cuff and gives her a cup of water.

Amelia flashes back to present time. He had done that to her a few times after that. She had to walk on eggshells until she found out how to leave him. Her amnesia brought her right back here. Looking in the room a bit longer, there's something else on the floor.

It's her phone. Why would my phone be here? Did he lie about losing it in the woods? She walks over to go through it. A lot of people texted her, she does have friends. Several of them asking why she's not answering. She then scrolls to see that Michael texted them, pretending to be her. He told everyone how she's doing fine and is not on her phone a lot anymore. Weird, she doesn't see a message from Dan. He must have deleted some messages that made him mad. She can't believe he kept this from her! Then, something else in her memory comes up. The person who pushed her.

She was on the trail, arguing with Michael again. Feeling fed up, she tried to leave him.

"I'm done Michael, you are the last person I'd want to marry! I can't even imagine having kids with a person like you. Would you give them the time-outs you give me? In a dark room, chained up? You're abusive and controlling."

"Shut up, I didn't spend all this time with you just to have you run off!"

He comes in really close, too close for her. She backs up as he keeps stepping forward. He continues to yell in a ramble and suddenly he loses it. She tries to walk around him to get from the edge, but he holds her there. She smacks his hands off and he yells out of frustration. Michael pushes her, hard. She turns to catch herself as she sees a tree. The rest is black.

Coming back to the present time she sits on the floor, becoming dizzy. It was Michael. Michael pushed me. I've been in a house with the guy who tried to kill me. Is he going to try and murder me again? She breathes heavy. Dan needs to get here fast.

Just as she thinks that, the front door opens up. Why would Dan just open the door instead of knocking? She runs to the stairs, and her mouth drops open. The door opened because it's Michael. He came home early.

25
Michael

The whole morning Amelia was acting weird, almost like she was in a hurry for some reason. Maybe she's trying to process the new rules I told her, but still, she seems different today. In his car, Michael keeps thinking of her odd behavior. The cameras will be in the house tomorrow, is she planning on doing something today? He tries to shake off his concern as he walks into work. After only an hour of work, his curiosity is at a high. She is doing something I don't know about. He goes to the receptionist and tells her to cancel his schedule for today. That he felt sick and was going home to get better. Getting back into his SUV, he speeds back to the house, convinced she's doing something wrong.

Opening the door to his house, he starts to look around for her. She hasn't cleaned yet, is she here? Michael looks back over at the stairs, she's quiet. Amelia is looking at him with wide eyes, like she's scared of him. His eyes shift down to her hand, where she's holding her phone. She went through the room. It was off limits, she knew that. Why does she choose to break my rules? He looks back up to her face, her green eyes filling up with tears. How is he going to fix this?

"Why do you have my phone Michael?" She waves it in the air for him to see.

"That's a new phone I got for you."

"No, it's not. Don't lie to me, why do you have my phone when it was supposed to be lost on the hiking trail?"

"Amelia, it's a new phone. Your confused with your amnesia. Why did you go in the guest room?"

"I'm not confused and you're not going to fool me. That's not a guest room either."

He tries to find the right words to diffuse the situation. "Amelia, I can explain –"

"You don't have to, because I already know. You're crazy and dangerous! You actually tried to kill me and then played it off like I was being clumsy and fell."

He freezes, she knows everything. "I wasn't trying to kill you, I swear! It was an accident. Sometimes I just get really mad and make mistakes, you know that. I never meant to hurt you, I just couldn't have you leave. I love you! I took you to the hospital. When they said you had amnesia, I thought we could start fresh. I would handle my anger better and you wouldn't remember the bad times we had. You weren't supposed to see that room. I was going to put that past us." He puts his hands out for forgiveness.

She stares at him for a long moment, her eyes wide open. "You're crazy and I'm leaving."

Amelia goes back to the room and comes out with a suitcase.

"Where are you going with that?" Michael starts to panic.

"Dan is coming to pick me up. He's not a person who tried to kill me." She continues to walk. He comes up and blocks her from moving any further. "Michael, move. I don't want you near me."

"I didn't try to kill you! And you can't go with Dan, you're my fiancée. You have to stay here, with me."

"I'm not your fiancée anymore." She takes off her ring and drops it on the floor.

Michael just stares at it. His sadness turns to anger. How could she just do that. After two years together. No relationship is perfect, but she just gave up. Amelia goes to walk by him, he puts his hand out to stop her. "I really wished we could have gone back to being happy and making each other laugh, but you won't let that happen."

"Let me go, I am not staying." She says in a sour tone.

He grabs her wrist hard to make sure she doesn't slip away. Michael picks up the ring and shoves it back on her finger. "But you are staying here. I'll deal with Dan when he comes by." She whimpers under his tight grip. "I don't want to have to use that room again, but I will if I don't think you'll behave tomorrow when other people come over."

She drops the suitcase and he bends over to get it. Michael throws it over to the kitchen, away from her reach, and turns back to her. She's not going to take control, I am.

"Let go that hurts!" Amelia tries to pry his hand open.

"No, I don't think I will. This is the consequence to your actions." He smiles at her.

She grits her teeth and knees him in the stomach. He lets go and bends over at the sudden force. Shocked, he processes what she did. Standing up straight, he feels the heat flow through him. She goes to run, but he snatches her long black

Amelia's Amnesia

hair and pulls her back in his reach. Michael takes his free hand and slaps her with the back of his hand. She falls to the floor and shields her face.

The heat continues to run through him. He kneels down over her.

"Are you going to stay?"

She spits in his face, wrong answer. Michael puts his hands around her neck and squeezes. Amelia immediately begins to squirm. His eyes go dark, emotionless. She takes her hand and scratches his face, digging deep into his skin. He lets out a grunt, letting his grip loosen with the pain in his face. He puts one hand up to touch the new mark on him, there's blood when he brings his hand back down to his eyes.

"You messed up my face!"

He watches her take her last breath in before tightening his grip again. His hair begins to fall out of place as he tries to keep her in place. She scratches at his arms and they both try to gain control. Her face begins to turn red and her hands start to move in slow motion. With her eyes flickering open and shut, Michael continues with what he's doing.

26

Brent

This is the last time Brent will be here. He knows Amelia is finally leaving Michael. He saw Amelia and Dan talk yesterday. Afterwards, he watched her plan what she was going to put in a suitcase. Brent can connect the dots. He's surprised Amelia forgave Dan after what he did, but I guess she's really desperate to get out of there. He still isn't worried about Dan, he's just a friend to her. Brent knows he is the one for her.

He watches her through the windows of the house, packing things as fast as she can. After all this time, he's happy that she will be single again. Things will be easier, Michael helped him out by pushing her away. Amelia finished packing early and now just stands in the bedroom. Brent's curious at what she'll spend her time doing. He soon regrets that thought when he notices her in the hallway, going towards the other room. She never saw it after the hospital. It would be better if she didn't.

He watches her go around the rooms looking for what he knows is the key. In the office, he sees her lift the key up, this will be hard for her to see. Amelia will definitely have some memories once she looks inside. Brent can't see much from his angle, but he has a good idea on what's happening. He knows what the room looks like as well, being in the house a few times. Brent also knows what she will find in there. Her phone, Michael decided to hide it in there while she was recovering at the hospital.

The day of the accident is still fresh in his head. Brent went to the trail to take in Amelia's beauty. He always wants to be near her. They were fighting though, pretty bad. Amelia wasn't holding back on how she felt about Michael, and he's not a man who can take rejection. Michael struggled to get back control. Brent being in the background, had no idea what to do. He could feel something about to happen, but he wasn't supposed to be there in the first place. Brent just watched, worried for Amelia, until it happened. Michael pushed her off the trail. Her head hit a tree, hard, and Brent heard her roll down the rest of the hill, receiving cuts and bruises on the way down. Michael held his head in his hands and let out a yell of panic. Brent thought she was dead, he would kill Michael. Seeing him run down the hill after her gave him some hope though. Maybe Amelia was hurt, not dead. Moving to another tree, he got a closer look at what was happening at the bottom. Michael kneeled down and checked her pulse. After a few seconds of silence, Michael lets out a deep sigh. She's alive. Brent then watches him as he grabs her phone that fell out near her head and hides it in his pocket. He so badly wants to come in and save her but knows now is not the time. Brent will help her later. Michael lifts her up and rushes off.

Dan should be here soon, she won't be at the house much longer. She can put all of this past her. As he has that thought, Brent sees a silver SUV pull up, it's Michael. What is he doing here? He should still be at work. Brent's adrenaline pumps up, Amelia's suitcase is packed and he will see that. He sees her at the top of the steps, and Michael at the door. Brent has perfect view of both of them.

The argument starts. It reminds him of her accident all over again. She needs to try and get out of there, Michael is starting to lose his temper. Brent feels useless, what can he do? Then it happens, Michael snaps. Brent can no longer look, he's freaking out. He can't wait for Dan to arrive and pick her up. He has to do something now.

Brent sprints from the woods to the house. This wasn't part of Brent's plan, but he has no choice. Last time was too close of a call. Michael will not take Amelia away from him. Michael is a problem that needs to be dealt with now.

27
Amelia

Her vision is flickering. She tries to hold on to the air she still has. Amelia didn't expect this from Michael. She regrets getting too close to him while arguing. As he cuts off her oxygen, she finds it harder to think.

In the background, she suddenly hears the door get kicked open and Michael's hands release from her throat. She looks up as she coughs to reboot her lungs. Dan just got here, he must have driven up in his car while we were fighting. Michael looks confused. "Who are you?"

Dan doesn't respond. He walks with purpose up to Michael as he tries to get up and spartan kicks him. The force sends Michael flying back, giving Dan the advantage. He continues to rush him, making Michael stay on the defense.

Dan lets out a smirk. "I've been wanting to do this for a while." He pushes Michael against the kitchen table and cracks him across the face with his fist. Amelia stays at the same spot on the floor, not daring to interject. Dan is taller and stronger than Michael, something Michael must not be used to. Holding his newly black eye, he leaves his ribs open, which Dan strikes with his elbow. Panicking, Michael turns the struggle around and wraps his arms around Dan's waist. Without hesitating, he lifts him up and slams him on his back. Having the new advantage, Michael punches him while he's stuck below him.

"No!" Amelia gets up from her frozen state and knees Michael in the face, helping her friend. Dan gets up. "Move, I don't want you getting hurt." Michael is stumbling around feeling disoriented. Dan goes over to finish their fight. He grabs his hair that is no longer slicked back and slams it against the fridge. That last blow was enough to knock him out.

Amelia feels relieved that it's over. Michael was going to kill her. Dan acted as her knight in shining armor. Maybe she does have some feelings for him that she hasn't been admitting to. Then, something dawns on her. "Why did Michael not know who you are?"

Dan turns from Michael to her. "What?"

"Michael asked who you were? He should already know you."

His face turns pale, something is wrong. Amelia takes a few steps back. She swears under her breathe when she notices her suitcase is closer to Dan than herself.

"I can explain everything." He puts his hands out, trying to show his innocents. She doesn't know what to think, not sure what to expect. She still can't trust her memory. Dan has a secret as well she doesn't know about.

"Please look at me. I'm not a bad guy."

Her worry grows stronger. "Why did he not know you Dan?"

He pauses for a moment, trying to tread carefully. "It's because I'm not Dan."

"Excuse me?" Am I dreaming? This can't be my reality.

"My name is Brent. I've known you for a year and pretended to be Dan so I could be close to you."

"If you knew me for a year, then why didn't you show up as yourself?"

He shuffles his feet. "You didn't know who I was. We've never talked."

Amelia connects the dots and takes more steps back. He's been following her. They weren't friends at all. Seeing her expression, he tries to explain more. "I was trying to find the right moment to meet you. It was always hard with Michael being in the picture. I always knew he wasn't the one for you, that I was. But you weren't going to see it that way, so I decided to wait."

She shakes her head in disbelief. "Is Dan even a real person, or is he made up?"

"Dan is real, and he is your friend. Michael told you to stop talking to him, even though Dan is interested in men."

"So this whole time you were acting as a completely different person."

"No, everything I said was true. Except for my name... and job. I'm a graphic designer. Our conversations and feelings were real. When I was Dan I was just your friend, now that I'm Brent we can explore our feelings for each other." He takes a few steps towards her.

"Feelings? I don't have feelings for you."

He cocks his head to the side. "Amelia, of course you do. I saw your mixed feelings. They weren't for Dan, they were for me. You were falling for me just like how I fell for you. We were meant to be together. I know it, and you will know it too. You can't tell me you didn't feel anything after we kissed."

Amelia's Amnesia

Her eyes are wide open. He sounds delusional. She tries to figure out what her next move should be. "How did you know me if I didn't know you?"

He smiles wide. "Through your romantic poetry. While I was working on my computer one day, I came across the website you worked for in my free time. The things you wrote were beautiful. It was like you were writing them for me, and we both live in New York. What are the chances of that happening? This is fate."

Forgetting the idea to grab her suitcase, she sprints for the door. Brent reacts fast and heads after her. The door is dented from his kick. Not needing to open it, she thinks she can make it. Amelia feels his arm wrap across her chest and another arm shut the door. She screams, reaching to open the door back up. He twists her around and covers her mouth, carrying her up the stairs. She kicks and screams, fearing the worst. Amelia would rather be around Michael at this point. Brent is just as dangerous, if not worse. Now she has to deal with a stalker. One that is carrying her up the stairs like she's a rag doll.

28
Brent

Taking his love up the stairs, he tries to think. Brent has no plan, everything happened so fast. When they reach the top, he chooses the bedroom. Brent closes the door and sits her down on the bed. She crawls to the opposite end of the bed, creating as much distance from him as she can. This was not what he wanted. He wanted their first time meeting to be special. Michael ruined that for him. I can still fix this. Over time I'll show Amelia that I'm a great guy. He tries to calm himself. She must be so scared after Michael tried to hurt her, she needs my help.

"Stay here while I find out what to do with Michael and then we will go from there."

She starts holding the covers up to her for comfort. "I want to leave."

"I know you want to. We can go as soon as I fix our problem."

"Go where? I want to leave by myself, without you."

He frowns at her. "I know this isn't the best way for us to meet but give me a chance. We're perfect for each other, you'll see. Now stay here and I'll be back."

Brent walks out the room. He grabs a chair out of the office and props it against the bedroom door to jam it closed. Just to ensure that she stays in there. He walks down to the kitchen, Michael is still laying in the same spot unconscious. What is he going to do with him? He can't kill him. That would definitely upset Amelia, and he's not a killer. For now I'll stuff him in a closet. He won't go to the cops, we know what he did. Brent goes to the garage and finds some duct tape. He rips off a piece and gets to work, first taping his mouth. He then wraps the tape around Michael's wrists and ankles. He wants him to have a difficult time freeing himself.

Brent looks at what he's done so far and decides to add some of the silver tape to the man's eyebrow. He will have a fun time pulling that off. Feeling content, he finds their coat closet and stuffs Michael in there.

Looking at his face one last time, he has multiple bruises, especially the large bump forming on his forehead where he hit the fridge. Brent doesn't care what he did to him, he deserved it. Maybe he will change how he acts with the next woman he dates. Michael can't have Amelia anymore, she's mine and I made that clear today. She was going to leave with me anyways. Remembering her suitcase, he goes back to grab it.

As he walks up to the glass wall in the kitchen, Brent sees a woman running towards the woods. It's Amelia. Dropping her suitcase, he runs back to the bedroom. The chair is still jammed against the doorknob. How did she get out? He opens the door and curses. The window is open with the bedspreads being tied in knots against the bed post. She climbed out using the sheets as rope. She's smart, he finds that sexy in woman. He can't have her go though.

Leaving the house, Brent runs after her, catching up fast. He knows these woods well, he's not worried.

29
Amelia

She darts straight towards the woods. When Brent locked her in the master bedroom, she saw the window as her only way out. Putting on grey sweat shorts and a white tank top, Amelia started creating her way out. She's desperate to get away from the only two people she knows. *How did I end up around these toxic people? One tried to kill me, and another is currently trying to kidnap me.*

Amelia hears Brent call after her. She was hoping she would have more of a head start before he found out. She reaches the opening of the woods and thinks about where she should go. Not the pond, he knows where that's at. She decides to go a random direction. The woods can't be that big, they live in New York, she'll eventually find her way out. Twigs crunch under her and branches scrape her arms and legs. Her hair starts hitting her face and she wishes she would have put it up before she climbed out the house.

She runs in zig zags, occasionally jumping over tree trunks or rocks in her way. Amelia hears him not too far behind her. Running hasn't worked in her advantage and soon Brent will close in their gap. She has to hide. Near a fallen, hollow trunk, she sees a spot where the ground slightly slopes down. Amelia crawls under the trunk and ducks down, pressing her body next to the trunk, making herself as small as possible. She hears footsteps close behind her, Brent stops running.

"I don't hear your footsteps anymore. Did you get tired?"

Covering her mouth, she doesn't dare respond. He continues his rant.

"I have water at my apartment. You can have some while you sit on my couch and I make us dinner. I know you're hungry baby, let's not do this game of hide and seek."

He walks around, looking around and under things. Every muscle in her is stiff, frozen in place. His footsteps are quiet, she can't see what's going on.

"Give me a chance. You liked Dan. Nothing's different, except we don't have to be friends anymore. We can finally be together."

Amelia squeezes her eyes shut, hoping this is just a long nightmare. One that she will wake up from soon and have all of her memory back. She wonders if she should run or stay. *If I try to run, he may catch me. If I stay hidden, he may find me.* Weighing her options, she decides to stay. Brent may walk off thinking she's in a different area.

"I never meant to freak you out Amelia. I just want you to come home, with me, where you along."

There's a long pause of silence. Moving her hand from her mouth, she slowly peaks under the tree trunk. She doesn't see any feet around her. *Maybe he walked off like I was hoping?* She waits a few more moments, looking under the trunk. Nothing.

She sticks her head under the trunk so she can crawl back out. She sucks in a breath of air when she feels a firm grip on her ankle. Trying to kick, she gets pulled back to turn around and see Brent's face. Amelia opens her mouth to scream, but he climbs over her to cover it.

"The only thing screaming's going to do is give me a headache."

She pushes her hips up against him to move him off of her. He stays his ground and she realizes it's no use. She's tired from running and no food. Seeing her give up, he continues to talk. "You can be cooperative and let me carry you back to the car, or you can put us both in panic and give me no choice but to knock you out. I really don't want to do that to you, especially when you have a lot of healing to do."

She glares at him. He hasn't really given her much of a choice. If Brent hits her like he did Michael, her head will only get worse. For now, Amelia will have to play along with him. Just until there's another way out.

"Okay, you're right. Let's go."

Brent leans down towards her. "You mean it, you want to come?"

"Yes, we can go. You can carry me Brent."

He smiles and kisses her forehead. "I knew you would come around. You'll love my place. I have it ready for you, so we only have to move in your stuff."

He picks her up with a boost of energy and keeps talking. "We're actually near my car. I have to park it away from your place when I come by to check on you. We can drive back to the house really quick so I can pick up your suitcase."

She looks into his blue eyes that are filled with light. This is a scary man. He thinks this is all normal. Amelia says nothing and continues to be carried.

Amelia's Amnesia

When they arrive at his red sedan, Brent pops open the trunk. She shakes her head. "I don't want to go in there. Let me sit next to you."

"I'm sorry, but this is only until I can fully trust you."

His steals a quick kiss on the lips, then rolls her in and shuts the trunk. It's completely dark. She slams on the top, but it doesn't open. Amelia hears the front door, and then the car starts. She can't believe she's in the back of someone's trunk. This guy is crazy, he's going to try and kill me like Michael.

She continues to bang on the top until her arms get tired. It's not going to open. She can't do anything right now, but eventually she will have an opportunity. Amelia has to be patient and find the exact chance she can get away.

30
Brent

He is driving back with a pep in his step. Everything is coming together. Amelia is still going back with him and she's coming to understand him. Brent knew it would just take her a little bit of time to process things. The sun is beginning to fall. She must be starving, not eating any lunch and the cardio she did today. He gets excited realizing they're going to have their first dinner together. I'll thaw some tilapia and grill brussels sprouts while she settles in.

Brent is almost at the apartments and thinks of how he's going to get her in there. His neighbors are always out at bars and parties, and for the first time he is thankful for that. He does not live in the busy city area, so they should have the right amount of privacy for tonight. He doesn't want to hide her like Michael, but he doesn't want any negative attention while she has to re-adjust.

He pulls into the small parking lot and stops his car. Brent walks over to the back with caution. He opens the trunk but leaves his hand on it in case it needs to be closed again. Amelia looks up at him, scared and unsure. He feels bad for putting her back there now.

"I'm sorry this is how we had to do things. We're here now, so I need to go over some things with you first."

She leans up on her elbows. "Do you have rules for me too?"

"No, they're not rules. Even though my neighbors aren't here I can't have you screaming and causing scenes. That won't be good for our relationship. I know this is a lot to handle, but you'll get used to it."

She arches her brow. "You can't be serious. You put me in the back of a trunk, and I have to smile about it?"

Brent is shaking his head. "I'm not saying to smile, just don't go crazy on me. Look, this will probably seem weird to other people if they see me talking to my trunk. I know you're hungry, can you come inside with me and I'll make us something. It's been a long day full of surprises. Let's just relax."

She glares at him for a moment more before agreeing and climbing out. His appearance looks calm, but he's ready to react if she tries anything. They both walk inside, and he pulls out the food. "Hey, I have something I want to show you."

"What is it?"

"It's sort of like a gift I guess. To show how much I love you."

She doesn't respond, so he takes her hand and directs her to his room. She is going to love the collage. Amelia will finally feel appreciated. As they arrive to the door, he stops her there. "Close your eyes."

"Okay." She smiles but has a nervous look behind it.

He holds her shoulders and places her in front of the collage. Brent lights a few lavender candles he placed there for when she would arrive. "Okay, you can open them." He has a bright smile on his face. Watching her face for every reaction. Her face goes from a closed smile to a puzzled look. "What's all this?" Amelia looks from one thing to the next.

"This is something I made for you." He goes and hugs her from behind, looking at it with her.

"Are these pictures of me? Did you take some of these without me knowing?"

"Well yeah, you're beautiful. Of course I want to take pictures of you." Brent lets her go so she can walk up closer to the wall.

"What are all of these poems, are they mine?" she holds a corner of the paper in her hand.

"Yeah, I fell in love with you because of these. You can continue writing them here now."

She turns her head to the next thing and covers her mouth. "Are these mine, or some other women's?" Amelia points to the black thong, not wanting to touch it.

"That's yours, I wouldn't have someone else's up here, or at all. It's something of yours that I find is very intimate and romantic."

She starts to step back in shock, it worries him. "Are you upset I stole them? I knew you would eventually be here. I can buy you new ones."

He goes to hold her, and she pushes him back. "Stay away from me, you're crazy!"

Brent lets out a laugh. "I'm not crazy, this is fate. Ever since I saw you and your emerald eyes, I knew you were the one. You are beautiful on the inside and out. You just need some time to see me the same way."

Amelia's Amnesia

He walks towards her and she continues to move away. Something in her expression changes. She seems to be more hostile, distancing herself from him. This isn't going to work between us. I need her near me, I did all of this for her. "Come here." He puts his hand out and she doesn't respond. She backs up even more.

31
Amelia

It's worse than what she thought. She tried to pretend and go with what Brent was doing. After seeing his room and what's in it, she wants nothing to do with him. He's obsessive, has he done this before? Brent continues to move towards her, Amelia continues to move away. Does he not understand that I don't want him near me, or does he not care? She feels like she's slowly being cornered and doesn't know what to do. I can't fight him, can I? He's bigger than me and I saw what he did to Michael. Not all of her wounds are healed.

"Amelia, stop moving away from me and come here." His tone has annoyance tied in it.

She hops on the bed to keep the space between them and he picks up speed and grabs her. She squirms, but he holds her there. "Stop this. I'm not some stranger, I'm your lover."

"No you're not! You are some psycho-stalker who can't except rejection!"

Brent pauses, his voice gets lower. "You don't mean that, you've had a long day."

She becomes furious, he's not getting it. "I do mean it. You're a creep! You keep saying this is fate and it's not. You don't love me Brent, you're obsessed! There's a difference. I do not want you, get that through your head. I will never want you." When she finishes, she watches his face.

Brent doesn't say anything. His expression is blank. He just looks down at her. She tries to get a read on him but can't. After a long minute, he gets up and leaves the room. She sits up, eyes wide. What is happening? He comes back with rope and a rag.

"What is that!"

He doesn't look at her. "I can't have you running off. Not when we're finally together."

Amelia panics. There is no way out after this, she needs to move now. She needs to fight now. Brent grabs her arm and she kicks him in the gut. His abs are hard, and she would have thought she didn't do much damage if he wouldn't have doubled over. Even though he's big, that doesn't mean he's invisible.

He looks up at her hurt, not physically but emotionally. "You hit me."

She goes to kick his face and he grabs her ankle. Amelia tries to kick with the other foot, and he throws her to the side. He stands up stiffer on his knees and slaps her in the face. A stinging sensation covers the side of her face. Brent is angry now, she can't turn back now. I might as well go all out. She gets up on her feet, runs across the bed, and spears Brent to the floor. Surprised, he gets the wind knocked out of him. She goes to run while he coughs, and he grabs her shin. Amelia trips and is back on the floor. He has faster reactions than I do. He crawls his way up her body and is on top again. She's at a disadvantage.

"Don't do this to me, I love you."

He looks at her with his sky-blue eyes. Gracing a finger across her face, he starts to nibble at her neck. Amelia let's out a scream immediately. He jumps at her reaction and covers her mouth. It doesn't stop her from screaming more. She swings her arms and legs, trying anything to get free. Brent sits up to try and calm her down and one of her fists connects with his face.

Instinctively, he puts his hand up to his face and she kicks him as hard as she can while he's distracted. Her foot meets his chest and he falls back. Amelia gets up again and runs out the bedroom. She's been going strong but is getting tired. Today has been an uphill battle. She gets to what she thinks is the living room area. Brent is up again and to keep a distance, she begins to throw things. She starts to throw books, small plants, the TV remote, anything that her hands can reach. He tries to either dodge them or block them. Brent slowly closes in the space and wraps his arms around her tight. She struggles to get out of his grasp.

"Amelia stop! This is ridiculous."

"Brent I can barely breathe." She points her face to the ceiling, trying to catch a breath. Her hair flowing down her back, moving as he sways her.

He throws her on the couch and holds her wrists down. He thinks I'm going to get tired and stop fighting, but he's wrong. This won't be over until I'm out of here. My life will not end here with him.

32
Brent

She is acting very stubborn today. He tries to keep his cool, but his anger is beginning to slither out of him. Brent is trying his best to not hurt her, even when she is trying to hurt him. He's not Michael. As he holds down her wrists, Amelia kicks her feet up at him. Brent sits on her to restrain her.

"You have got to calm down. Stressing this much isn't good for you. Let's make this be a good night for us. I saved you from Michael."

She groans out of frustration. "Tonight is not a good night. You only saved me from Michael for your own selfish reasons. I'd rather be around him right now then you!"

"Don't say that! He's a terrible person who tried to use you as a trophy wife. I did all of this for you!"

"You're a terrible person! I never asked for any of this. If you were normal, maybe we could be friends, but that's it! You need help Brent, I feel sorry for your past girlfriends."

His anger begins to boil up to the surface. He can feel his face get hot. "They don't understand how to be loved! I thought you would, but maybe I was wrong. I waited a whole year for you, because I love you!"

Amelia grits her teeth at him. "You mean nothing to me."

His anger snaps. Brent stands up, grabs her by the neck and lifts her to her feet too. Just as he lets go of her neck, his other hand punches the side of her head. The force carries her to the floor. She doesn't move, doesn't get up. He can see blood coming down her forehead where her stitches used to be. His anger is replaced with panic. *Did I just kill her?*

He stands in silence, she still doesn't move. Brent kneels down next to her and lifts her head. Blood runs down his arm. He tears up. "No, I'm so sorry! I didn't mean to. You need to come back to me baby. I don't know what to do without you!" He goes to check for a pulse on her neck. She's still beating, it's not even faint. He looks at her puzzled and a small flowerpot from one of the plants she threw came crashing down on his head.

Feeling dizzy, he moves back. His vision gets blurry as he tries to find his surroundings. Brent watches the figure of her leave and come back with what seems to be his laptop. With a hard swing, she hits him over the head again before everything goes black.

33
Amelia

Brent is laid out on the carpet. She is relieved but is not sure how long he will stay that way. She fishes through his pockets and grabs his cell phone. Amelia dials 911 and frantically tells the operator everything that has happened today. She leaves out the rest of what's happened, knowing that would be too much information for them to follow. The only thing she needs right now is some help, she can tell her story later.

Amelia opens the door and it is dark outside. She sits down and waits out there, in case she needs an exit to run from. Minutes later, an ambulance shows up with a police car behind it. She stands up and waves to them. Wondering why the paramedic looks concerned for her, she remembers she's still bleeding. She must have forgotten with her adrenaline running. She looks down at her tank top that is barely white anymore. The dirt brown color is now mixed with red, dripping from her forehead. She lifts her hairline up for the paramedic to get a better look at it.

The woman leads her over to the ambulance as the cops walk into the apartment, guns to their side. In the light, Amelia can see that the paramedic is a woman in her mid-thirties, very pale. Her brown hair runs down her back in a tight braid and her face is spotted with freckles. The woman is speaking, but she can't process what she is saying. She looks at the woman putting on gloves and sees a gorgeous ring on her finger. Amelia looks at her own finger, forgetting that she had been wearing Michael's engagement ring this whole time. Taking it off, she drops it on the parking lot gravel, ending that chapter of her life.

The paramedic flashes the light at her eyes and she shut them because of the sudden brightness.

"Ma'am, can you hear me?" The woman is looking directly at her.

"Yes, sorry. I'm still trying to process everything."

"Can you tell me what happened to your head?"

"The guy in here hit me where I had just gotten stitches a few weeks ago. It broke the stitches open."

"Stitches?" The paramedic examines the cut again. "What did you need those for?"

Amelia explained her fall and the amnesia she had gotten from it. Although she was feeling fine. The woman told her that she had to go to the hospital overnight, because of her conditions. After she had her forehead patched up and disinfected, two detectives walked up next to her.

The woman was pretty, her hair in a tight bun. She felt bad for how the other detective must be tired, having bags under his eyes. "Hello Miss, I am Detective Burgh, and this is Detective Smith. I would just like to ask you a few questions while you are still here at the scene. Do you have a name?"

She smiled back at them. "Yes, I am Amelia Jones. I do not remember much in the past weeks though, because I have been in an accident that caused me to have retrograde amnesia."

The detectives looked at each other. Why would they do that?

"Ms. Jones, we were assigned to your hiking accident. We met your fiancé, Michael Williams."

Amelia shook her head. "He's not my fiancé anymore."

They both looked at her puzzled, and she began to explain everything. Detective Smith wrote down everything she said. Amelia told them how Michael pushed her, hid her phone, the creepy room he had, how Dan was Brent, and how Brent recently kidnapped her to try and keep her.

"Wow. That is quite impressive how you handled all of that. I am sorry you had to go through all of that Ms. Jones." Detective Burgh is shaking his head.

Detective Smith adds on to the conversation, her voice is smooth and relaxing. "What we will do now is send you to the hospital. Detective Burgh and I will stay on watch until Michael is picked up as well to put your mind at ease."

Amelia smiles. "Thank you. Could I also have my phone back? I'm going to need to find out where I can stay after the hospital." She has no idea where she can go.

"A friend of yours named Jasmine Porter has called into our office. She was wondering where you were at, but at the time we could not assist her. Since the circumstances have changed, I will call her and see if she would like to help. She said you two used to be roommates before Michael came into the picture."

I had a roommate? That was something no one told me about. Amelia feels better now that there's a plan in place. She looks over at the officers and paramedic coming out of the apartment. With the officers, is Brent. He's back up, walking with hand cuffs. As he walks to the cop car, they lock eyes and she gets a chill down her back. It's over now, things will be better now.

34
Amelia

Being in the hospital, it feels different this time. She's not aching or confused. Amelia feels at peace, the toxic people are out of her life. The same nurse she had last time insisted she be assigned to her again.

"I can't believe that Michael boy. He fooled the both of us." The fragile nurse rants as she checks her vitals.

It didn't take long for the cops to find Michael. He was banging on the coat closet door, still tied up in duct tape. Michael and Brent are currently being held in county jail. Detective Burgh and Detective Smith believe they will find enough evidence to put the both of them away for a while.

Amelia turns her head towards the sweet nurse. "I never got your name last time I was here."

The nurse smiles with her pink lipstick lips. "I'm Nurse Ruby sweetie." She flashes Amelia her name tag.

"I'm glad I have you to look after me Nurse Ruby." She gives her a sincere smile.

"Honey, you are just the cutest thing. I'm going to miss you, all you needed was an overnight stay. Your friend Jasmine is coming soon to pick you up." The nurse pats her shoulder.

Amelia is excited to see her friend. After Detective Smith talked to Jasmine, she jumped at the opportunity for them to be roommates again. She spent the whole night cleaning her place up and getting it ready.

About half an hour later, Amelia sees a woman pop her head through the doorway. The woman sees her and squeals out of excitement as she rushes over to hug her. This must be Jasmine. Having no needles in her this time, Amelia hugs her back. She is a gorgeous woman in her mid-twenties who could turn heads. Jasmine has black hair with thick braids that reach her waist. She has curves like Amelia and full lips as well. Her complexion is dark, and her skin is smooth. All she wears is mascara, and that's all she needs. She is wearing a purple blouse with a grey pencil skirt. The two of them together could get any man's attention.

Amelia looks back up at her face. She is wearing a big smile for her friend she was so worried about.

"I never trusted Michael. He always had this look on his face that made my stomach turn." Jasmine hugs her again.

Amelia pauses. "I remember you, at least some of you." She sees the apartment they lived in. They would do everything together, like sisters. Jasmine is a vet-tech and animal lover, with a dalmatian named Brutus.

"I'm going to help you with all of that. Detective Smith filled me in on everything." Jasmine hands a bag to her. "I pulled out an outfit for you from my closet. We're basically the same size."

Amelia changes into the red short sleeve hoodie and black leggings. They both leave in Jasmine's blue SUV. She lives closer to the city than Brent and Michael. Amelia is happy to be around people again. When they walk in, Jasmine gives Amelia her phone and goes through everyone. She then pulls up her social media and they go through all of the pictures. For Amelia to be back with her friend feels refreshing.

The two of them get in touch with all of their friends, including the real Dan, to have a party. Amelia will eventually regain her memory with the help of Dr. Mart, but she also wants to make new ones with her friends Michael has kept her away from. She is finally free and happy.

Epilogue
Brent

In prison, Brent lays on his bed. He looks through his box full of Amelia's pictures. *The timing just wasn't right. I shouldn't have rushed things she wasn't ready for. It was too much for her to take in at once.*

He has some time to spend behind bars, but on good behavior he hopes to get out a little early. He won't forget Amelia while he's in here, he will never forget her. She is the love of his life. People want to keep them apart, but that won't happen, he won't let it. Fate is stronger than a restraining order. They will be together again, married with children. *Her pregnancy will be beautiful, holding my children.* They will have a puppy as well to play with her and the kids. He kisses one of her photos and goes to look at another one.

He's been waiting to get a visit from her. she hasn't come by yet, but he's patient. *Good things take time*, Brent thinks to himself. She's worth the wait, the woman he was meant to be with.

He continues to work out and look good for her. She deserves to be next to a good-looking man. *Amelia thought I was handsome before, and I plan to keep it that way. She will eventually be mine, but for now I'll wait. I'll plan everything out and it will be perfect.* He knows he's right and she will learn within time.

Brent sits up and writes Amelia another love letter. Pouring his heart out and adding her own quotes from her poetry. She hasn't replied, but he's okay with that. *My letters are so moving, she probably doesn't know what to say.* Once he's done with the letter, he reviews it. "You will be mine." He kisses it and waits.

Acknowledgments

I am grateful for Dorrance Publishing, who helped make this possible. I would like to give thanks to Rebecca. She gave me guidance on how to go about creating a book step by step. Lance, who read and helped edit my book. He was with me through the whole process. I also want to give thanks to all my friends who believed I could do this, even when I wasn't sure